PO

Laura didn't like and didn't trust Dan Harland, and she couldn't understand why her grandfather thought so highly of him. It was obvious that Dan wanted to take control of the family firm—and her grandfather was actually encouraging him to marry her as a means of doing so. And she was horribly afraid that Dan didn't just want possession of the firm; he wanted her too . . .

*Books you will enjoy*
*by CHARLOTTE LAMB*

### DARK DOMINION

The marriage of Caroline and James Fox had run into serious trouble after only a short time—and the situation was not helped by the fairly obvious fact that James was involved with another woman. But would anything be improved if Caroline turned to her old friend Jake, who made it clear that he wanted to be more than a friend . . . ?

### TWIST OF FATE

Much as she loved her beautiful actress mother, Joanne could see that Ben Norris had a point when he considered her 'no better than she ought to be'—but he had absolutely no right to assume that Joanne was that kind of girl as well. Yet why should she care one way or the other what Ben thought of her?

### DARK MASTER

'I'm offering you an escape and a salve for your pride,' was Philippe de Villonne's way of proposing marriage to Alex after her fiancé had let her down. She accepted—then realised how foolish she had been to leave love out of the bargain. Was it too late to put things right?

### TEMPTATION

Joss White had been the first man—and the first love—in Linden's life, but he had treated her callously and broken her heart and then gone away, and she could never forgive him. Then they met again. Would Linden be foolish enough to turn to Joss again, knowing that if she did, she would hurt Daniel Wyatt as she herself had once been hurt?

# POSSESSION

BY
CHARLOTTE LAMB

MILLS & BOON LIMITED
17-19 FOLEY STREET
LONDON W1A 1DR

*All the characters in this book have no existence outside the imagination of the Author, and have no relation whatsoever to anyone bearing the same name or names. They are not even distantly inspired by any individual known or unknown to the Author, and all the incidents are pure invention.*

*The text of this publication or any part thereof may not be reproduced or transmitted in any form or by any means, electronic or mechanical, including photocopying, recording, storage in an information retrieval system, or otherwise, without the written permission of the publisher.*

*This book is sold subject to the condition that it shall not, by way of trade or otherwise, be lent, resold, hired out or otherwise circulated without the prior consent of the publisher in any form of binding or cover other than that in which it is published and without a similar condition including this condition being imposed on the subsequent purchaser.*

*First published 1979*
*Australian copyright 1979*
*Philippine copyright 1979*
*This edition 1979*

© *Charlotte Lamb 1979*

ISBN 0 263 73082 4

*Set in Linotype Baskerville 11 on 12 pt.*

*Made and printed in Great Britain by*
*Richard Clay (The Chaucer Press), Ltd., Bungay, Suffolk*

# CHAPTER ONE

Laura sat down, smiling at her flatmate, Renata, then yawned, making Renata laugh. 'What time did you come in last night?'

'Goodness knows,' Laura laughed, picking up a letter which lay beside her plate. She grimaced over it. 'Jimmy! Now what's wrong, I wonder? He only writes to me when he wants to complain about Marcus.' She put it down and poured herself some coffee, took a croissant and buttered it.

Renata had worked for Laura's family firm in England. She knew Jimmy Belsize and her answering shrug was eloquent. 'Coming back to Switzerland with me was the best thing you've ever done! You are better off out of the squabbles which go on between your father and grandfather ... I have never known such a family!' She watched as Laura quickly read the letter. 'What bees has he got in his bonnet now?'

Laura frowned. 'The new director—Harland—Dad seems to suspect he's taking over the firm.' The letter was hysterical, full of uncompleted sentences and wild accusations, but that was nothing new. Her father was prone to sudden fits of rage and suspicion, and she had learnt to take his outbursts with a pinch of salt. Normally she would have sighed over his letter and waited for what was bothering him to blow over, as it always seemed to do. His moods never lasted long, although they could be violent while they lasted. But something in the depth of his hostility towards the unknown Dan Harland struck her as more than usually bitter.

Her blue eyes darkened. Jimmy, she thought with a deep sigh. Why was he the way he was?

'Harland?' Renata pursed her lips as she poured herself another cup of the excellent coffee. 'I did not meet him.'

'Neither did I,' Laura confessed. 'He took his seat on the board after I left London. He came highly recommended from Sir Lionel Joseph, I seem to remember. My grandfather always listens to Sir Lionel ... they're old buddies from the war years.' She folded the letter and pushed it into her handbag, getting up from the breakfast bar in the tiny kitchenette with a long sigh. 'Oh, I've no doubt Dad is blowing his top over nothing again. Sir Lionel is usually sound on the men he employs, and in my last letter from Grandfather there was no hint of any trouble.'

'You know your father,' Renata smiled, her pale blue eyes dancing. She was a very thin girl, quite tall, her movements stiff and precise. 'I grew to be quite fond of him, but he is filled with jealousy, isn't he? Anyone your grandfather likes becomes the target for his suspicions.'

It was true, and Laura groaned. 'Sharp girl! Poor Dad. He's never got over the fact that Grandfather refuses to hand over the firm to him lock, stock and barrel.'

Jimmy Belsize had nobody but himself to blame

for that, she thought. He was no fool, yet he had frittered away his earlier years in the firm, taking advantage of his position to absent himself whenever he felt like playing golf, flying off to Paris, pursuing his latest girl-friend. Growing up without a mother, Laura had often resented her father's constant succession of women, but she had learnt to turn a blind eye to them, realising in time that they meant no more to him than the pleasure of a moment. He had never married again. His florid, broad-shouldered good looks attracted women in droves. He spent money freely. But she doubted if he had ever cared much for anyone since her mother died.

His playboy attitude had been responsible for his father's distrust of him, and although he remained one of the company's top executives, Marcus Belsize had never agreed to promote him to the position of managing director, continuing to hold it himself. Jimmy had bitterly attacked his father for that, claiming that Marcus just would not let go of his power.

'He'll hate giving up even when he's dead,' he had said to her once. 'I've no doubt if you could come back from the grave, he would.'

She had winced at that, looking at him gravely. She loved her father, but she could not help seeing the justice of her grandfather's view of him.

'Don't whine, Jimmy,' Marcus had snapped once, and her father had turned crimson, his eyes glittering under his heavy brows, but the words had stayed with Laura ever since, somehow characteristic of both men, both of her father's sullen, suspicious shallowness and of her grandfather with his brusque tongue, heavy glare and assertion.

In her year away from Belsize & Company she had felt a new freedom, a lighthearted pleasure in her life which was novel to her. Renata had introduced her to a fun-loving crowd among which she had met several attractive, attentive young men. None of her boy-friends had become close enough to be regarded seriously, but in their way each had been a pleasant companion, and their company had made the year pass quickly. She liked her job. She was good at it and well paid. She always had something to do in her leisure time.

She was by no means eager to return to London. In his letter, her father had begged her to do just that. 'Come home,' he had said, 'before Harland steals your bread from your mouth.'

How could he do that? she asked herself, sighing. Her father was, as usual, reacting with exaggerated alarm. No doubt he and the new director had had some little row, and Marcus, when Jimmy ran to complain to him, had been irritated and taken the other man's side. She had seen the pattern before.

Going to work, she put the whole problem out of her mind. She had a new boy-friend, a charming, dark-eyed Swiss whose company soon banished her father's querulous complaints from her mind. She had seen him rather a lot lately and Renata had asked teasingly, 'Can it be true love at last?' Laura had laughed, light of foot and of heart. 'We're going dancing tonight,' she had said. 'Have you noticed his black eyes? And those gorgeous teeth?'

'Teeth,' Renata had said wickedly, 'are the last things I notice in a man!'

A week passed and Jimmy's letter was forgotten. Her handsome Swiss took her to a party, and she wore a swirling black velvet skirt with a red silk top whose very low neckline was tied with a fringed tassel. 'And what happens when I pull the tassel?' he enquired, and she gave him a teasing look. 'Pull it and see.' He looked into her wicked blue eyes and said smilingly, 'I am too cowardly—I suspect the roof would fall on my head!' Laura grinned at him. Although she made a gay, lighthearted companion she never had any trouble fending men off—she had inherited some of Marcus's hauteur, although she exerted it only when she chose to do so.

When they returned that night it was almost three in the morning. Max opened the flat door for her and then kissed her hard for a long time, his mouth warm and expert on her own.

'Let me come in for a coffee,' he whispered, his arm still round her waist, and she breathlessly shook her head.

'Renata will wake up ... no, goodnight ...'

Reluctantly he kissed her again and walked away, and she closed the door, leaning against it, laughing softly under her breath, because it really had been the most wonderful evening.

And then the light clicked on and she opened her eyes wide, feeling like someone in a spy film when they are trapped under the searchlights and do not know where to look. 'Renata?' she asked, bewildered, and then her dazed eyes saw a movement in the room, and focused on the tall, black-haired figure facing her.

There was a curious hiatus as though neither of them knew what to say, staring at each other across the room. She slowly absorbed his six-foot height, his wide shoulders, the evening jacket he was wearing, the strong cold face beneath the black hair, coming at last to meet the grey eyes which surveyed her in her turn expressionlessly.

'Who are you?' she asked at last.

He came forward then and held out a well-shaped brown hand. 'Dan Harland, Miss Belsize,' he said, and her eyes snapped open wide.

So this was Dan Harland, she thought with curious appraisal. The whizz-kid imported by Marcus to stiffen up the board, her father's arch-enemy at present, and with just a brief knowledge of this man she could guess why Jimmy detested him. They would be chalk and cheese. This was no jovial drinking companion for Jimmy's idle hours, no man to chat with on the golf course or in a bar or swop telephone numbers with when one was visiting a strange city. This man was ice from his well-polished shoes to his sleek head.

It was almost with reluctance that she gave him her hand, and she withdrew it almost at once after a brief touch. 'What are you doing in my flat?' she asked, and then with sudden alarm, 'Is something wrong? Marcus?'

It had to be Marcus, she thought. He was seventy and although he was very strong, both physically and mentally, he was an old man.

But Dan Harland shook his head. 'No, Marcus is fine,' he said, still studying her with those cold grey eyes. 'Won't you sit down, Miss Belsize?'

She lifted her dark head, eyes wary. 'No, thank you,' she said quietly. 'Just tell me, will you? It's Jimmy, then.' If it was not Marcus it had to be her father.

The grey eyes watched her as though for signs of

strain, for some telltale signal which would indicate that she was volatile explosive which might blow up in his face. She was, after all, Jimmy's daughter, and no doubt he expected her to be of the same nature, but she wasn't. She knew that. She was Marcus's granddaughter, and although she was slender and fine-boned she had steady eyes and a firm mouth.

'Tell me,' she repeated flatly. 'I'm not going to have hysterics.'

'Your father has had an accident,' he said then in even tones. 'He was driving on the motorway and went through to the other carriageway.'

How typical, she thought. As throughout his life, Jimmy had been going the wrong way, heading upstream in the teeth of all sense.

Aloud she asked calmly, 'Is he badly hurt?'

Dan Harland nodded. 'I'm afraid so. They've taken him to a hospital nearby which specialises in road accidents. He'll have the very best of care.'

Of course he would, she thought irritably. She would never doubt that. Marcus might find his son infuriating, but he would pull out every stop to make sure he got the best of care.

'Multiple injuries?' she asked in careful tones. From the sound of it, Jimmy was lucky to be alive at all, but then if Marcus had been concerned enough to send Dan Harland here to get her, then perhaps Jimmy was not alive for long. Perhaps that explained the man's presence. He had been sent to bring her home in time to see Jimmy die.

She lifted her large velvety blue eyes to him, the thick black lashes curling back from them and leaving them very wide. 'Is he going to die?' she asked without inflection.

He considered her thoughtfully. 'Off the top of my head I can't be sure,' he said. 'Given luck and a certain amount of will to live, he should pull through. It all depends upon him.'

She looked down almost dazedly at her evening clothes, at the dangling cord which her handsome young Swiss had insisted on playing with during dinner, teasing her with it. 'I must change,' she said. 'What time is our flight?'

'I booked one for six o'clock in the morning,' he said. 'I wasn't sure what time you would get home.'

She laughed, faintly ironic. 'No,' she said, her lower lip shaking a little. 'Get yourself a drink while I change.'

He watched her impassively as she walked into her bedroom. When the door had closed the tears came, and the silent rush was like a tap being turned on. She stood there, trembling, pressing her lips together to make sure no sound emerged which could alert the man in the other room. She leaned on the wall, unable to stop the flow for the moment. The tears felt hot as they forced their way through her closed lids and when at last they stopped her eyes felt hot as though someone had rubbed sand in them.

At last she straightened and softly trod across the room, splashing her wet face with cold water, gently dabbing it dry. Then she stripped off her clothes and took a cool shower, her head safely covered with a plastic shower cap. She dressed in a charcoal grey suit she wore for the office usually, the pleated skirt fitting her small waist like a second skin and falling mid-calf. The tiny waistcoat gave interesting formality to the frilled lace of the jabot and long lacy cuffs. She brushed her hair to a neat, shining bell around her face, applied fresh make-up and after a final satisfied glance, went out of the room.

Dan Harland got up from his chair, a glass in his long hand, and ran those impassive eyes over her. He really was a monolith of a man, she thought. He gave nothing away.

'Have you eaten?' she asked him, and he nodded.

'Your flatmate cooked us both a meal,' he said.

Her eyes widened and a glint came into them. 'Really?'

'Very kind of her,' he added, and she gave him an amused, slightly taunting look.

'I'm sure she was happy to do it,' she said meaningly, but there was no answering light of amusement in his grey eyes. He merely nodded as if agreeing with her courteously.

No sense of humour, she decided. 'I have to pack a few things,' she told him, looking at the tiny silver watch Jimmy had given her for her fourteenth birthday. It was still her favourite piece of jewellery, the delicacy of the filigree bracelet enchanting on her white skin. 'It's three o'clock. We'll have to be at the airport an hour before the plane goes, so I'll do it now. I'm sorry to keep you waiting so long. You should merely have rung from London—I could have caught the plane alone.'

'Your grandfather didn't want you to hear the news over the telephone, Miss Belsize,' he said.

'Did you volunteer or were you pressganged?' she asked, tongue in cheek.

'It was my own suggestion,' he said.

'How terribly thoughtful of you,' she said sweetly, and her eyes held a sudden hostility because he had been her father's enemy and she could imagine, looking at that ruthless face, that he would be a bad enemy to have. Whatever his reasons for coming over to Geneva to fetch her, they would have nothing to do with kindness, generosity or concern.

Renata's bedroom door opened suddenly and she drifted in, still half asleep, her usually pale face flushed with sleep. 'Oh, Laura darling,' she exclaimed, holding the lapels of her wrap together. 'I'm so sorry about your father ... I would have waited up, but Mr Harland told me that he would cope and I felt so sleepy.'

Laura brushed her cheek lightly. 'Forget it, pet,' she said. She was fond of Renata. She knew that her friend would have waited up had Dan Harland given her the slightest encouragement to do so. Judging by the faint animosity of Renata's glance at him, she could guess that he had frozen Renata to bed hours ago. 'Come and help me pack,' she said, and they both went into the bedroom and closed the door.

'He's been here for hours,' Renata whispered. 'He wanted to go and look for you, but I had no idea where you and Max were going ... he asked me a lot of questions about Max and he made a few phone-calls trying to track you down ... clubs and hotels ... but we never found you.'

'We were at a party,' Laura explained.

Sidetracked, Renata asked, 'Good, was it?'

It had been fantastic, but it seemed now to have been a dream. She could barely recall the mood of dreamy euphoria which had wrapped her as she came home. Dan Harland's news had shattered it, and she thought with brief sadness of Max whom she might very likely never see again. That could have been the start of a very beautiful friendship. 'Very good,' she told Renata. 'And you? How did you get on with our Mr Harland?'

They were both packing expertly, neatly, quickly, moving from wardrobe to suitcase and back again. 'He's impossible,' said Renata, lifting a pile of silken lingerie from a drawer. 'I cooked him supper and he ate it very politely and sat there saying nothing until in sheer self-defence I went to bed.'

'What, no passes?' Laura asked mockingly.

'Not even an elementary one,' said Renata. Then she looked at Laura anxiously. 'And your father? He is very poorly?'

The use of the word brought a lump to Laura's throat and a faint sob to her voice. 'Not too good,' she said.

'Which is English understatement for very bad,' Renata guessed with a sigh. 'I am very sorry, darling.'

'Yes,' sighed Laura, snapping the case shut. 'I'll send for the rest of my things. Could you pack them up? See to my office farewells for me?'

'You will not be coming back.' That was statement, not question, and Laura smiled at her affectionately.

'It's been a fantastic year and I'll miss you very much.'

'Me, too,' said Renata. 'Poor Max ... a very brief romance for him, I'm afraid.'

Laura gave a wry smile. 'You can have him with

my love. He likes rum chocolates, by the way, and is a super dancer.'

Renata had opened the door and Laura's voice floated out as Dan Harland stood up. Walking into the other room she caught the flash of his grey eyes, a peculiar twist of his mouth, as though, hearing her last words, he was inwardly commenting with irony on her casual bestowal of her boy-friend on her flatmate.

Who cared if Dan Harland disapproved? she thought, returning his stare with a cold look of her own. She kissed Renata, who patted her on the back, clinging.

'Write,' Renata muttered.

'Of course. And you.' Conscious of Dan Harland's listening ears, Laura added in brittle tones, 'Kiss Max for me and good luck with him. Just watch his hands. I think he's got six!'

Renata laughed and groaned. 'I hope your father's all right.'

Dan Harland had opened the door and was waiting with a patience which was deliberate, visual, underlined.

Laura walked past him and he took her case from her hand. She turned her head and felt tears prick her eyes as Renata waved to her, then they were stepping into the lift and Renata had vanished.

While they waited in the half-empty, echoing airport she drank several totally unwanted cups of strong coffee and listened to the boom of the tannoy voices as they announced flight delays and departures with equal enthusiasm. Dan Harland sat there in a black overcoat, a knee crossed over, one black shoe-cap swinging in her angle of vision.

'Why are you wearing evening dress?' she asked, suddenly registering the fact.

'I was dressing to go to the theatre when I heard the news,' he explained. 'I got a flight at once. I was lucky—they had a seat on the first plane out.'

'What a pity,' she said politely. 'What were you going to see?'

He looked at her as though she were a caterpillar which had just crawled into his lettuce. 'A new play,' he said shortly.

'Do you often go to the theatre?'

'No,' he said, and that was that. He had no intention of making small talk, she could see that, and she could see, too, why Renata had slunk off to bed. She studied him thoughtfully through her long curling lashes. He was handsome, in his cold way, with the powerful physique of the natural athlete, and no doubt in the normal way Renata would have been delighted to sit up all night with him if she had had any encouragement.

She looked at the black windows glittering in the electric light. Morning was just coming up in the east, a pale red glow streaking the sky. There was something unreal about the fact that she was sitting here in this great chrome and glass building, hearing the marble floor echo with passing feet, the boom of the tannoy, the occasional throb of aircraft taking off, and opposite her this stranger in his formal, expensive evening clothes. There was a surrealistic feel about the whole scene. In England her father was lying in a hospital bed, perhaps dying, and she might never get there in time, and she was not crying, she was sitting there making polite small talk with a man she detested.

She got up and made her way to the cloakroom and looked at herself in the mirror above the washbasin after she had dried her face. She must stop crying. Her eyes were distinctly pink around the rims and she would look like a white mouse.

Jimmy would not die: Marcus would not let him. She clung on to that. Marcus had a will of iron. He would fight for Jimmy if Jimmy would not fight for himself, and at that she was touching the crux of the matter, because she had a terrible feeling that her father was not going to fight to live.

He had never fought for anything. He had taken what life gave him and complained when it did not give him all he wanted, but he had never gone out and fought for anything.

He just would not know how to fight. Her eyes ran over again and she felt like slapping her own face, but instead she dug her nails into her pink palms until blood sprang in five little crescents and the tears stopped.

When she walked out to join Dan Harland as the flight was called she looked totally in command of herself, a slender, graceful girl with smooth black hair in her elegant charcoal grey suit. The smooth matt complexion showed no signs of tears. The blue eyes might be a little bright, but that could be the lighting.

He made her sit by the window and watched as she clicked her belt home. 'You must be tired,' he said. 'Try to sleep.'

She looked at him and by now she really hated him, because had she had anyone else with her she could have given in to the sorrow which was threatening to engulf her at every moment, but under this man's cold, expressionless eyes she could only force back the tears and bear it. She silently closed her eyes, and, because she was exhausted and sick with grief she fell asleep almost at once. It was a troubled, tossing sort of sleep in which she was almost on the point of waking all the time, shifting in her seat, her brows frowning, her breathing impeded.

At one point she twisted her hands around her seat belt, struggling in her sleep to untie it, almost as though she felt it was the belt which was disturbing her.

Dan Harland leant over and gently lifted her hands free, and his touch woke her. Her eyes opened and she stared at him, but he was not looking at her, he was staring at her palms with that expressionless face. Embarrassed, hot, she closed her eyes again and felt him lay her hands down on her lap before he sat back in his seat. What on earth must he have thought, she asked herself, seeing the dark red marks of her nails in her skin?

She slept again, too weary to do anything else, and when he shook her very softly her eyes opened with reluctance, staring up with bewilderment in the first moment of waking at his hard-boned face, the features so absent of expression that he could have been a statue carved in some strange stone, his eyes half-veiled by heavy lids.

'We've arrived,' he said, and she snapped back to life with a pang of sick misery. Her lids flickered as she reasserted her calm.

She sat up as the plane landed with a faint jolt, then taxied smoothly to a stop. 'Did you sleep?' she asked him for want of something else to say.

'No,' he said.

'You must be worn out,' she said brightly. 'You can't have slept all night.' Did he run on electricity like a machine? she wondered.

'I took a nap while I waited for you,' he added.

'Sitting up in a chair? Clever stuff.' Her voice was sarcastic and she made no attempt to hide it.

'It's a knack,' he shrugged.

'Oh, empire-winning behaviour,' she said, and she was making fun of him because he annoyed her so much, and that was how he struck her, to be honest, as a man who ruled empires and was unflappable, a master of himself and ruler of others. Not a very likeable man, she told herself, not a man to whom one could run if one had made a mistake. He would not forgive easily. He would not forget.

'We've a car waiting for us,' he said as he carried her case for her as they left the airport. It was crowded here in London, the morning rush was under way, people with frantic, bored faces tearing around with the look of mesmerised fugitives.

The car was there, as he had prophesied, and God help someone if it had not been, Laura thought, as she sat back beside him and the limousine gathered speed towards the motorway.

'Are you hungry?' he asked. 'Would you like to stop and eat? We have quite a journey in front of us, remember.'

'No, thank you,' she said politely, a well-mannered child, her face cool and empty. 'I'm not hungry.'

'Well, I am,' he said, and the bluntness surprised her. She looked at him with widening eyes.

'Of course—I'm sorry.' It had not entered her head. He looked like a man who ate nails for breakfast and the thought made her lips twitch. Do motorway cafés supply nails? she wondered. And am I getting hysterical?

He shot her an odd look as if the same thought had entered his head. 'We'll stop when we see somewhere suitable,' he said.

They stopped at a pleasant enough place, but the food was greasy and Laura felt sick, so she merely nibbled at a roll and butter, drinking hot coffee which made her stomach heave. Dan Harland eyed her meal with a grim face.

'That won't settle your stomach,' he said, and she wondered if he knew her stomach was like a washing machine, irritated at the thought that he might know anything about her at all. She did not want him to have a clue about her. She wanted to be faceless and anonymous to him.

'I don't want any more,' she said firmly, staring back at him with a defiant look.

They drove onward and she was beginning to feel so tense that she was knotted inside like a coiled spring, her hands clenched into fists, held at her side as she sat upright and stiff beside her companion.

It was spring. Some of the trees were alight with new leaves, their curled green buds bursting from the black wood like tiny fireworks. The morning sky was a calm milky blue, tender and filled with diffused light from the invisible sun behind the clouds. It streamed in rays from the edge of one riven cloud, reminding her of a painting by Blake, and she wondered if God was behind it with spread hands, illuminating the universe. A handkerchief was suddenly pushed into her hands and she started, turning her smooth head to stare at the man beside her, a man she felt she had never looked at before, so much had his movement taken her by surprise.

Her dazed bewilderment was obvious, and he leaned over and gently took the handkerchief again, wiping her wet cheeks with it. She sighed, closing her eyes, and he drew it across the pink lids, his touch so soft she barely felt it.

The car slewed and she fell with it, caught by him, supported, her slender body graceful in his arms. She heard the cool thud of his heart under her ear, then he pushed her back into her seat and she gave him a brief smile. 'I'm sorry.'

He slid his handkerchief back into his pocket.

'Give that to me,' she said. 'I'll have it washed.'

He did not seem to have heard. 'We're here,' he said, and she looked out with horror at the rows of windows, the ugly functional buildings, the parked cars and neat, empty flower beds.

'Yes,' she said flatly. 'We're here.'

She shivered as she climbed out of the car, although the spring morning was bright and fine. He put a hand beneath her elbow and she moved away, refusing to be supported. Upright, she walked into the foyer and heard him speaking to someone, his deep cold voice clear. 'This way,' he said to her, and she followed him blindly.

Hospitals have their own particular atmosphere; hushed, as in a church, ordered, as in a school, their air redolent of disinfectant, polish, anaesthetic, pungent scents which only come together in one place. Nurses walked quietly with shoes with rubber soles. The wheels of invalid chairs squeaked. Trolleys rattled. Vases of flowers stood, dehumanised, outside swinging ward doors.

Dan Harland ushered her into a small waiting-room and there was Marcus, looking smaller, frailer, older. Laura ran into his arms and clung with trembling hands, crying, and Marcus patted her shoulders, muttering words she never heard.

Then she was removed from him with the firmness of a nanny removing a fretful child, and seated, while Marcus sat down beside her and Dan Harland stood above them, watching them both with those austere eyes.

She gave him a look of hatred. Then she looked at Marcus and was shocked by his pallor. 'Jimmy ...' she whispered. 'Is he ... ?'

'Holding his own,' Marcus said faintly. 'The operation is over and he's in an intensive care unit. They say it's touch and go.'

'Have you slept tonight, sir?' Dan Harland asked him, and Marcus looked vague.

'I'm fine,' he said.

Dan Harland looked at him, then went out without another word, and Laura pushed her hand into her grandfather's, feeling the knotted frailty of his with a sensation of compassion and alarm. Where was the oaklike strength she had known all her life? This was an old man sitting beside her, and she felt bereft and helpless.

'You should get some sleep, darling,' she said. 'You can't do anything here and they would let you know if you were needed.'

'I'm fine,' he said obstinately, then Dan Harland came back through the door with his carved cold face and his strength, looking at Marcus searchingly.

'I've spoken to the doctors,' he said. 'Jimmy will sleep for a day, at least, and they say you should go home now. They'll call if they think you should come back.' He bent and lifted Marcus as easily as if the older man was a child, taking his arm when he was on his feet. 'I have a car outside. I'll take you both home.'

Marcus made no further objections. They were driven home and Marcus slid into a faint doze on the way, waking with a snort as they came to a stop. His housekeeper, Mrs Jacques, came running to meet them, her face upset. 'How is he?'

'Holding his own,' said Marcus, as he had said to Laura.

'Take him to bed,' Dan said to the housekeeper quietly, and she put an arm around Marcus's waist, steering him away, but he stopped and turned to look at Dan with weary eyes.

'Thank you, Dan,' he said in a husky voice. 'I don't know what I would have done without you to rely on.'

'I'll take care of the office tomorrow,' Dan told her. 'Don't even think about the firm. You can leave it all to me.'

'I know,' said Marcus, sighing. 'Thank God! I rely on you, Dan.' He went out and Laura stood there, staring at Dan Harland, and knowing now precisely how much her father had had to go on when he spoke of this man's menace, because she had seen the utter reliance in her grandfather's white face, the trust, the belief, and she was suddenly afraid. Marcus was pinning his hopes upon a man without feelings. She knew that, just looking at Dan Harland. He was ruthless, totally objective, cold, logical, efficient. No doubt he made a first-class second-in-command, but if his icy brain demanded a human sacrifice she had no doubt he would produce one. He had no emotions. For the present he was Marcus's right-hand man. Very soon he would have control of the firm. And then he would shed Marcus and Jimmy without a second's hesitation, because his cold, clever brain would tell him of the necessity, and he would have no emotional weakness to stop him. He was like a tank without a brake. He would roll on remorselessly over the living and the dead and nothing would stop him.

## CHAPTER TWO

JIMMY'S face was swathed in bandages through which his eyes gleamed dimly as Laura bent to smile at him. 'I can't even kiss you,' she said sadly. 'You look like a mummy. How do you feel?'

'Fed up,' he croaked rustily, and she laughed because even to hear that unrecognisable voice was something after he had lain unmoving and silent day after day.

'Poor darling, of course you are. I've bought you some tapes ... your favourite dance band! That should cheer you up.' She unpacked the things she had brought him, laying the fruit in the great bowl, while he watched her wryly.

'Don't look like that,' she soothed. 'Sister said you could start to eat fruit in a day or two.'

'Through a straw?' he asked, and although she could see nothing of his face she could hear the discontent in his tones.

'Jimmy, be patient ... it won't be long! It's a miracle you're still here with us after that accident. You've been very brave and good, and you'll get your reward.'

'Sorry you had to be dragged back from Geneva,' he said, and although it was a mock apology she heard the accusation behind the words and looked at him kindly.

'I would have come back soon, anyway.'

'Get my letter?' He sounded sharp.

She nodded, looking at him closely. 'How much of it did you mean?'

'All of it,' he said, shifting angrily, and she laid a hand on his bandaged shoulder warningly.

'Don't! Keep still ... you mustn't get upset or Sister will make me go.'

'I want to talk,' he said. 'I have to ... Laura, baby, the man's a threat to both of us ... you, as well as me. He's after the firm.'

Gently she said. 'Dad, how can he be? You know the controlling shares are in Marcus's hands. The family holds the voting balance. How can an outsider influence that?'

'Marcus ...' Jimmy muttered, and she could tell he was becoming upset again. 'Marcus will give it to him.'

'But, Dad ...'

'Baby, he will!'

'Marcus would never leave those shares to anyone outside the family,' she said firmly.

'In trust,' he said, and his voice was tired. 'In trust

for you, baby, but controlled by Dan Harland.'

Laura was silent, seeing it then. 'Has Marcus told you so?'

'Hinted,' said Jimmy. The gleam of his eyes vanished as he closed his lids.

'You're tired,' she murmured. 'You must sleep ... don't worry, Dad, I'll speak to Marcus. He wouldn't want to hurt you, hurt either of us,'

Jimmy sighed and she went out, quietly closing the door. As she drove home she was thinking hard. Jimmy's accusation might have some foundation if what he said was true. The Belsize company had gone public some years earlier. Forty-nine per cent of the stock was held by the public while the controlling fifty-one per cent was in Marcus's possession. It had always been understood that at his death those shares would descend to her father and thence to her, but if Marcus had decided that he could not trust Jimmy with them he might well have decided to bypass her father by leaving the shares in trust to her with Dan Harland as executor.

A frown creased her forehead. She was twenty-two now. Even if Marcus did as he threatened, surely the trusteeship could not last more than a few years? And what could Dan Harland do in such a time? He would have no right to sell the shares; he could only control the firm during his trusteeship.

She had been living with Marcus during Jimmy's long pull back to health. When she got to the house she found him reading his newspaper in his favourite chair, his face tired. Looking at him with compunction, she noticed how old he seemed since Jimmy's accident.

He looked up, smiling. 'Laura, how was he?'

'Better,' she said, coming over to kiss his wrinkled forehead. He looked pale, she thought. Worry had aged and worn him.

She sat down on a stool beside him and held both his hands in her own, the smooth black bell of her hair falling from her face in a shining wave. 'Grandfather, Jimmy is worried, and I don't think worry is good for him while he's still so ill, so I promised to talk to you.'

Marcus looked secretive, his face suddenly wary. 'What about?'

'Dan Harland,' she said, and Marcus made an irritated noise with his tongue.

'Jimmy has taken one of his dislikes to Dan, but let me tell you, Dan is the mainspring of the firm right now. If it wasn't for him, God knows what would have happened to the company with Jimmy crashing like that.'

'Jimmy suspects that you intend to put the family shares into a trust with Dan Harland as executor,' she said bluntly.

Marcus leaned back, his neck trembling slightly, his head swaying like an old tortoise's. 'Maybe that's in my mind,' he said slowly. 'The shares are mine, Laura. I've the right to do as I choose with them.'

She drew an unsteady breath. So Jimmy had not been guessing in the dark! Her enormous blue eyes remained steadily on Marcus's face. 'Have you actually done this, Marcus?'

'Is this the third degree?' He pulled his knotted hands out of her grasp and sat up, his eyes angry. 'The firm is mine. I built it up. I'm not sitting back to watch while Jimmy smashes it the way he smashed that car of his.'

'But, Marcus ...'

He stood up angrily. 'I refuse to discuss it any further. It's my business how I choose to leave my money.' He walked to the door, paused and looked back at her grimly. 'It will all be yours one day, Laura, don't fret about that.'

'I don't give a damn for myself,' she snapped, her temper flaring to meet his. 'I'm worried about my father. You're hurting him!'

His face softened slightly, he sighed. 'Don't try to salvage Jimmy, my dear. He's a lost cause.' Then he went out and she sat there, staring at nothing, her face white and troubled. There was a weakness, a vulnerability, about Jimmy which tore at her heart. He would never be able to stand on his own and no doubt Marcus knew precisely what he was doing when he took any hope of running the firm away from him, but at this moment in time it would be a tragic blow to Jimmy.

She had seen nothing of Dan Harland during the past few weeks. Her time had been spent largely in looking after Marcus and visiting her father, but now that Jimmy was getting better she felt it was time she began to think about her future. She left it for a few days and then spoke to Marcus over breakfast.

'Go back to work?' Her grandfather looked at her shrewdly. 'Getting bored, my dear?'

She smiled, her eyes faintly teasing. 'Of you? Of course not. But I like to feel I'm a working girl, you know. I've no intention of drifting into a life of leisure.'

'Your old job with the firm is being very capably done by someone else, Laura,' he said. 'But I think we could find you something else.' The tired eyes surveyed her thoughtfully. 'After your year in Switzerland you're in line for promotion, anyway. Give me a few days to think it over, will you?'

Laura had gone into the firm after her eighteenth birthday, having no interest in an academic career, refusing to go to university. She had taken a secretarial training during her last year at school and had progressed rapidly at Belsize & Co. There was never any need for her grandfather to push her. She was quick, cool-headed, efficient and hard-working.

The firm owned a large number of hotels around the world and she had worked on various aspects of the administration with the work. The departments interlocked so that each one she joined was another piece of the puzzle, slowly forming a picture for her of the way the firm ran.

During her year in Switzerland she had perfected her French and German, both tongues being spoken there, and through her job with one of the hotels the Belsize company owned she had learnt the rock-bottom base of the business, seeing things from the other side of the fence. Her grasp of the firm was wide and confident. At the back of her mind had always been the knowledge that one day she might be in control, but now it looked as though that control would for a long time be in the hands of Dan Harland.

Three days later Marcus informed her lightly that Dan Harland was coming to dinner. 'Wear something pretty, my dear,' he said with a very innocent expression, and she looked at him sharply. What was he up to?

She took care, however, to do as he asked, choosing

one of her more expensive dresses, a sophisticated sheath in midnight blue with an overdress of black lace which erupted at the low neckline in a flurry of foaming waves pinned with a pale pink rose. Expertly cut; it clung to her slender figure like a second skin.

When she came down to dinner she found Dan Harland there with her grandfather. Both men stood up as she came into the room and she came to kiss Marcus, who beamed at her approvingly. When she glanced at Dan Harland, however, she found no intimation in the cold face of how he reacted to her appearance. He inclined his head. 'Miss Belsize.'

'Come now,' Marcus said brightly. 'Why so formal, Dan? Call her Laura!'

The grey eyes flickered very slightly. Laura met their glance without batting an eyelash.

She waited for him to speak, but he said nothing and with irritation she realised that he was forcing her to speak first, insisting that it was up to her to second her grandfather's invitation to use her first name. Dan Harland had no intention of begging her for anything.

Her features tightened. 'Please, do call me Laura,' she said with a false sweetness, her blue eyes vicious.

'Thank you,' he said in that deep, cool voice. 'May I get you a sherry, Laura?'

'Thank you,' she said, longing to behave outrageously, hit him, insult him, anything to make that carved blank face show some reaction.

He moved to the decanters and her eyes followed him, staring at the wide dark-clothed shoulders, the strong line of his body; firm waistline tapering to lithe hips, the chest moulded to his crisp white shirt, the long muscled legs which moved with such assurance, as though he were physically in the peak of condition. As a male specimen he was quite unquestionably superb.

'Do you ride?' she asked, and he looked over his shoulder, the turn of that powerful head making her stomach tighten.

'Horses? Yes, when I have time.'

'Play golf?'

'Rarely,' he said.

'Dan plays squash and fences three times a week,' Marcus volunteered. 'He likes to keep fit, don't you, Dan? Wise man.'

The glass of sherry was put into her hand and the grey eyes met her own briefly. 'What do you do to keep fit, Laura?' He used her name with an odd deliberation, as though he were mocking her by the use of it.

'She plays squash,' her grandfather said with an eagerness which took her aback. 'You must give her a game some time, Dan.'

'I doubt if we're evenly matched,' she said drily.

The grey eyes looked at her over the rim of his glass. 'Shall we find out?' he asked, and Laura sensed something more behind the question than a polite invitation to play squash. 'How about tomorrow morning?'

Marcus looked delightedly at her. 'Yes, Laura, I can spare you tomorrow.'

She flushed angrily, feeling that she had been manipulated into this but not certain why she should feel so reluctant.

'We'll have lunch afterwards,' said Dan Harland, and the invitation was so phrased that she could think of no courteous way in which she could decline.

During the dinner she was careful to speak to him with the quiet courtesy of a stranger, her eyes never dwelling on him for more than was necessary from sheer good manners. Marcus had had a very good wine sent up and the meal was excellent, but she found her appetite was small and barely touched her food. Once Dan Harland glanced at her plate and then at her, eyes narrowed in speculation, but he made no comment.

They drank their coffee in the drawing-room, but Marcus claimed weariness as soon as his first cup was drunk, and withdrew, leaving Laura with the unenviable task of talking to Dan Harland alone. It was, she thought grimly, like making polite conversation with one of the circle at Stonehenge. He sat there, his body casual yet sheathed in that terrifying power, watching her, and her mind went blank.

To her enormous relief, Mrs Jacques came in and announced a telephone call for her. 'From Switzerland, miss,' she said, excited, and Laura quietly excused herself to Dan Harland and went off to the phone. It was Max, sounding aggrieved because she had not contacted him since she left.

'I'm sorry, Max, I've had so much to worry about,' she said, and he was comforting at once, his voice warm.

'I miss you,' he told her. 'When are you coming back?'

'Never,' she sighed, and he erupted in concerned questions.

'My father was so badly hurt . . . I can't leave him.'

'Then if Mahomet will not come to the mountain,' he said in a vainglorious way, his voice determined, 'I shall be flying to London soon. I'll expect to see something of you then.'

She laughed. 'Yes, Max. Goodnight!'

He blew her a kiss and she teasingly blew one back, replacing the receiver with a smile on her face. Poor Renata! So Max had not turned to her for comfort. It was flattering, but she was in no mood for love at the moment and Max was yet another complication of a very complicated situation. She turned, still smiling, and found Dan Harland in the room, his hands in his pockets, watching her with those expressionless eyes.

'I must be going,' he said, before she had a chance to ask what he thought he was doing, eavesdropping on her private conversations. 'I'll book a court for tomorrow at eleven. Will you meet me at the office?'

She nodded curtly and he was gone before she could think of any reply.

Laura was under no illusions about her chances against him, but the crushing defeat he imposed on her next morning was humiliating. She looked with dazed helplessness at the lean, powerful figure in brief white shorts and shirt as he swooped and struck, the ball ricocheting off the wall with the force of a thunderbolt, giving her no possible chance of touching it. He made no concessions. He was playing to win and she hadn't a hope of stopping him.

There was more to it than that, though, and they both knew it. He was demonstrating to her just what she was up against with him. The physical strength he showed her was symbolic. If she attempted to take him on in battle for the company she would lose: he meant her to know that. The cold grey eyes underlined it for her as he stood, his towel around his brown neck, watching her as, heaving breathlessly, she leaned against the wall.

She closed her eyes, fighting for breath. My God! she thought, he's half killed me. It was like playing against a machine.

She opened her eyes and felt colour rush over her body in a hot wave as she found him looking at her slender figure in a fashion which was unmistakable. His eyes lifted to her face and they stared at each other. She was shaking.

Dan took a step towards her and she shrank visually, horrified. She felt like some rabbit under the eyes of a predator. This man stalked and struck and there was no escape.

He turned away and walked out, leaving the door open. She looked around the stark, white-walled room as though she had just escaped some frightful fate in it.

She was not an inexperienced adolescent. She had often been the object of male admiration, approval, even passion, but never before in her life had she stood, shuddering, while a man looked at her as Dan Harland had looked at her. The cold, unemotional sexual assessment in those grey eyes had left her chilled and angry.

He had inspected her body from head to toe in slow appraisal, as though she were for sale. Her hands clenched at her sides. How dared he? Having inflicted that crushing defeat on her he had then insulted her.

'Swine!' she said aloud, and the word echoed in the bare room like a warning.

She slowly followed him and went into the changing rooms, showering with intensity, as though trying to wash off the touch of those cold grey eyes.

When she rejoined him she was immaculate in a lime-green dress with white collar and cuffs, her face as expressionless as his, her eyes completely under control now.

They lunched at a small French restaurant. Laura carefully ate her meal, not wishing Dan to know he had taken away her appetite again. Just as they reached the coffee stage he leaned forward and said coolly: 'Marcus tells me you want a job.'

Her black lashes curled back. 'Yes,' she said, meeting his stare, the blue eyes defiant.

'When could you start?'

She was wary. 'Right away,' she said slowly. She would put no obstacles in the way which he could use against her.

He took his time in lighting a cigar, staring at the end of it, his face empty. When it was well alight he blew a fine wreath of blue smoke into the air and glanced at her through it. 'Monday suit you?' he asked.

'What is the job?' she asked.

His eyes watched her. 'My assistant,' he said.

The shock made her stiffen. What was he playing at now? Was he setting her up for another humiliating defeat? She stared at him and got no clue from that monolithic face.

'What exactly would that entail?'

'Doing what you're told,' he said bluntly.

Her colour deepened to a creamy pink. 'Of course,' she said with sarcasm.

His lids dropped, the dark lashes flickering, and

she wondered what lay behind them, what he was hiding from her.

'Could I have a few details?' she asked coldly. 'A few hints as to what I would be dealing with?'

'People, largely,' he answered, and the lids flew open, revealing the grey eyes suddenly glinting with an icy humour which startled her. 'You can do that, can't you, Laura? Charm and coax the men I'm doing business with? Talk sweetly to them on the telephone ... keep them dangling when I'm in no hurry ... promise them paradise and then cut the thread and watch without wincing while they fall through a hole in the world?'

Her cheeks burnt with a fierce red, her eyes hated him, because they both knew that he was not merely talking about work. He was making an oblique comment on other things. He was getting at her.

She was angry enough to retort sharply. 'Oh, I think I could manage that,' she snapped, glaring back at him.

'Of course you could,' he drawled. 'Exercise your natural talents.' His eyes flicked over her slender body and back to her furious face. 'Of which you have many, I'm sure.' And again the sarcasm bit into her, maddening her, because she had no answer to any of this—she had handed him this weapon without thinking when she let him hear her talking of Max to Renata, when she talked to Max on the phone.

This man used whatever came to hand. He found the weapons other people carelessly left about, and he used them without remorse.

She stiffened her backbone and gave him a mocking smile. 'I've never had any difficulty in coping with men,' she confessed, reversing the weapon, using it against him, showing him that she did not fear it and hoping that that would make it useless to him.

He looked at her through his lashes. 'You don't need to tell me that,' he said. 'I'm very observant.'

'I'm sure you are!' Bright, casual, unconcerned, she let her eyes drift over him in a deliberate simulation of how he had looked at her earlier. 'And I'm sure you're very talented yourself.'

She had wanted to anger him. Instead she had amused him, and that annoyed her. He laughed, showing those even predatory white teeth. 'I must prove that to you some time,' he drawled, and the reply brought a clenched sickness to her stomach, as though something was coiled there, a snake of physical reaction which appalled her.

She had never had a conversation like it in her life. Anyone listening might be excused for imagining it to be idle chit-chat, but it was a fight to the death, in deadly earnest, and she hated and feared him.

She glanced at her watch with a light exclamation of mock surprise. 'Good heavens, is that the time? I must be keeping you from your work and we can't have that, can we?'

He looked coldly amused again. 'No,' he agreed, rising and giving a click of the fingers to the waiter. He walked with her to the door after settling the bill and helped her into her short jacket. The touch of those long, strong fingers on her bare neck made her shiver with repulsion and shock.

How could she possibly bear to work with him day after day in close proximity? She could not bear to be in his company now for more than a few hours without wanting to take a gun to him.

She drove to the hospital to see Jimmy and told him about the job as Dan's assistant. Jimmy looked excited, his eyes glinting. 'Now that's good news,' he said. 'You keep your eye on him, baby. We'll stop that swine if it's the last thing we do. Keep as close to him as you can. Don't let him do a thing you don't know about ... there must be something we can do to stop him.'

She thought of the powerful, lithe figure smashing her all over the squash court and she inwardly doubted it. Dan Harland was inviolate, untouchable. Neither she nor her father had the strength to fight him, and Marcus was too old.

'I'll do my best,' she promised, and Jimmy put out a limp hand to take her own gratefully. The weakness in his grip made her heart ache. She bent and kissed him. 'Now that the bandages have gone you look more human,' she said. 'I'm kissing a man, not a mummy.'

'They won't give me a mirror,' Jimmy complained, staring at her with fever-bright eyes. 'Am I very scarred?'

He was, and she did not know how to tell him, because he was so volatile, so easily disturbed. 'Your skin will heal,' she soothed. 'Give it time.'

Plastic surgery, the doctor had told her, was the only answer, but Jimmy was in no condition to hear that; he would take it badly.

'When do you start work for him?' he asked.

'Monday,' she told him, and her tone was grim. She was not looking forward to it. She felt like someone on the brink of the unknown, shivering in her shoes, because Dan Harland could do her terrible damage, and she was scared stiff of him, which was a first, because never in her life before had anyone or anything scared her like that. She had always been a calmly confident girl, even as a schoolgirl; she had been born with a golden spoon in her mouth and the security of her background had given her unshaken certainty in herself. She had never been in love in her life, but she had loved. She loved Marcus and Jimmy. She had been in and out of bright infatuations as a girl, but they had none of them really touched the cool central core of her personality. They had drawn her like candles drawing a moth and she had always fluttered away, wings unsinged. Now she was afraid and she was not even certain what it was she was afraid of, only that Dan Harland constituted a threat to herself, although it was possible that it was all a mirage conjured up in her brain by a weird combination of events. Jimmy's hysterical letter, combined with the shock of his accident, might have built Dan Harland up into an ogre in her mind. Then she thought of his cold speculative eyes in the squash court and she shivered. No! There was more to it than simple hysteria.

Jimmy's eyes went to the door and there stood the Sister in her dark blue uniform, her face calmly chiding. 'I'm afraid you must go now, Miss Belsize,' she said. 'He must rest now.'

Jimmy's lip pouted. He looked sullen and yet appealing, a very large, teddy-bear-like man in his hospital pyjamas, the web of scars merely making him pathetic and sweet. 'What else do I do but rest?' he asked the Sister, who shook her head at him as if he were three years old.

'Now, now, we have to do what we're told,' she said, and Laura stifled a grin at hearing Jimmy spoken to like that.

She left him bewailing his fate and the Sister, reverting to a human persona, said, 'When he leaves us he must spend some weeks convalescing somewhere quiet. Will you and your grandfather think about it?'

'Can you suggest anywhere?' Laura asked, and the woman grimaced.

'A children's hospital,' she said with wry humour.

'Is he very childish?' Laura laughed, and the woman laughed, too.

'For a man of his age, unbelievably,' she said. 'Sometimes I feel like giving him a slap, but then he's still very sick.'

'Frankly,' said Laura, 'he's always the same, but I'll speak to my grandfather about the convalescence.'

'It will be months before it happens, though,' the Sister warned.

Laura nodded, sighing. She went back to Marcus, who was bright-eyed with eagerness as she joined him. 'How did it go?' he asked, and still thinking of Jimmy she began to answer him, but he curtly said, 'Not that ... Dan.'

She stiffened, looking at him shrewdly. 'He offered me a job as his assistant.'

'You took it?' Marcus looked at her hopefully and she nodded.

'I took it.' That Marcus earnestly desired her to take the job was obvious, but what was not so clear were his reasons for wishing her to be working beside Dan Harland. It could be merely that he wanted to be sure she was deeply involved in the firm, learning the job, ready one day to take over control, but she felt her instincts pricking. By the pricking of my thumbs, she thought grimly ... but what exactly was it that she felt so strongly threatened her?

Marcus was her grandfather. He loved her. She did not doubt that, even now, looking at him with that pleasure in his face because she had accepted a job with Dan Harland.

What harm could be meant to her if Marcus wanted this so deeply? She looked at him and wished she could ask and be sure he would reply frankly, but she did not feel sure he would. He would hedge, evade, refuse to give a straight answer.

He and Dan Harland were planning something. But what?

That Saturday she found Dan Harland dining with them once more. This time Marcus had not warned her, and she came down to dinner unprepared for the sight of that lean, hard figure seated opposite her grandfather in the drawing-room. She halted in the doorway and they both looked round at her.

She was wearing a rose pink dress, full-skirted, tight-waisted, her shoulders bare, her long, slim legs golden beneath the shadow of the hem.

'Are you going out?' Marcus asked, and there was open disappointment in his voice.

She came further into the room. 'Yes, I have a date.'

'Who with?' he asked, frowning.

'Joe,' she said, and was surprised when his frown deepened, because Joe Laxey was an old friend of the family, an attractive man in his early thirties, his business flourishing, his eligibility making him quite a catch for anyone. Marcus had once beamed when Laura went out with Joe. While she was in Switzerland she had seen Joe once—when he came over on business and rang her up. She had never been in the slightest bit in love with him, but she enjoyed his company and knew he liked her.

Suddenly, it seemed, he was no longer smiled upon, and she gave Marcus a sharp, questioning look.

Dan had risen politely and was clearly waiting for her to sit down. She would have taken a chair some way away from him, but as she walked towards it he took her elbow with the very lightest of pressures and she angrily found herself seated beside him on the long brocade sofa. Like a conjuror producing a rabbit from a hat he proffered a glass of Martini and she took it, fuming.

'Can't you put him off?' Marcus asked her in fretful tones, surprising her, because he had never once interfered like this in her private life.

She shook her head, sipping her drink. 'Of course not! He has tickets for a play.'

'Are you dining here first?' Dan Harland asked, and she looked at him with reluctance because she was finding it more and more difficult to face him, although she could not put her finger on the reason for her deep reluctance.

'Yes,' she said curtly.

'Then no problem,' he said lightly. 'Is there, sir?' And looked at Marcus, who looked back for a moment without speaking, then sighed and said unconvincingly, 'No, no, of course not.'

She saw the look they exchanged and the hair bristled on the back of her neck. She swallowed some more of her drink to cover her sudden heat. So, she thought, that was it ... she should have seen it earlier, but it had never entered her head, nothing had been further from her mind, but now she knew and she was appalled.

Marcus and Dan Harland were planning her marriage. To Dan Harland. She saw it in a blinding flash. All her moments of suspicion jelled into this ghastly realisation ... it was the answer to everything, both for Marcus and for Dan Harland. It would keep the firm in the family possession and yet give control of it to Dan Harland.

Over my dead body, she thought grimly. Oh, God, over my dead body!

## CHAPTER THREE

WHEN Joe arrived to pick her up after dinner, she took him in to say hello to Marcus and he was greeted very politely yet with that undertone of mild discouragement, and Joe was quick. He picked it up. He glanced at Dan Harland's watchful figure and met the steely gaze of those eyes with interest.

Picking her wrap up from the chair where she had dropped it, he laid it around her slender shoulders, smiling down into her face. 'Ready, then, sweetheart?'

'Ready,' she said lightly. 'Goodnight.' She threw the word between her grandfather and Dan Harland without quite looking at either of them, then she and Joe left, and in the car Joe asked quietly, 'What's going on, Laura? Marcus was a bit uptight. Not bad news of Jimmy, I hope?'

'Just business,' she said. 'You know Marcus ... when the business is on his mind he has no time for anything else.'

'Something wrong?' Joe asked, and because obviously she could not have him imagine that anything was wrong at the firm she shook her head.

'Oh, no, it's merely a small problem of personal relations.'

'Harland's running the firm now, I hear.' Joe heard everything. He was very well informed.

'For the present,' she agreed, and if she had her way it would be the shortest run of management in the world. When she thought of what he and Marcus planned for her she wanted to scream. How Marcus could do this to her!

Joe made a good companion. His broad, casual figure had a stocky reliability which was comforting, and he had kind brown eyes, like a dog's, warm and steady. They got on together. Conversation never flagged. They knew each other well and there were no emotions to cause any hang-ups in the talk. Laura enjoyed the evening very much.

'I've got to go to Stockholm next Wednesday,' he said. 'When I get back I'll give you a ring.'

'I'd like that,' she said, and she knew she would always be glad to see him. He was a nice man, but in her year in Switzerland she had barely thought of him except on that occasion when he came over there and they spent an evening together.

On the Monday morning she began work for Dan Harland, and she chose her dress very carefully, efficient without being striking, simple, pale grey, nun-like with a neatly rolled collar and wrist-length sleeves. It was pouring with rain, so she wore Russian-style boots with fur bindings in strips at the top, and her matching coat with the enormous fur collar and full skirt.

She was shaking her umbrella before dropping it into the rack when Dan Harland walked into the office.

He inspected her from head to foot in a lightning glance. 'Come through when you're ready,' he said, walking past.

She made a face at his back, hung up her coat, ran a comb through her hair and walked in after him. He was seated in his swivel chair, some letters in his hand, and he glanced at her boots with lifted brows.

'Wear shoes in the office, please,' he said curtly.

'It was raining,' she snapped.

His grey eyes were ice floes. 'I'm aware of that. I prefer you to wear shoes. This isn't a farm.'

Her colour rose. She closed her lips on the retort she was about to make. 'Yes, sir,' she said sarcastically.

He leaned back, placing the letters on his blotter and staring at her expressionlessly. 'Let's get one thing straight,' he said. 'I run this firm.'

'For the present,' she corrected, bitter triumph in her eyes, because he had given her that opening and she was overjoyed with the chance.

His lip curled. 'What makes you think there's any time limit?'

She threw caution to the winds. 'My grandfather will leave the shares to me,' she said with confidence.

'Ownership is not possession,' he returned, and for a moment she had to think about that, work it out. Her face reflected her anger.

'In time, Mr Harland, I will control this firm.'

He smiled almost wearily, as though she were merely tiresome. 'In time, Miss Belsize.' But not yet, his tone told her, and not for a long time.

He picked up the letters and handed her two. 'Deal with these, will you? Both get the same treatment... we're interested but we need time to think. Charm and tact, Miss Belsize... that's what I want from you this morning.' And his eyes were mocking as he said it.

She snatched the letters and whirled to leave. 'And change your footwear,' he said to her back. 'Shoes, please, in future.'

As she flung open the door she heard him add softly, 'I like to see your legs.'

She had closed the door before those words registered and then she stood still, seething. Pulling herself together, she made a study of the two letters and then made the phone calls necessary, soothing down the impatient clients, promising speedy decisions, charming them into a contented cooing.

She was summoned back to Dan's office later and sat in a chair in front of his broad, leather-topped desk while he swung thoughtfully in his chair and filled her in on the projects they were currently dealing with in the office. She listened intently, nodding. The telephone rang halfway through and he broke off to answer it in his crisp, cold voice.

The tone changed and she looked up, alerted.

Dan was staring down at his blotter, doodling on it with a pen, drawing a perfect rose, the petals delicately outlined with quick strokes. 'Olivia, my dear, how are you? Oh, fine, thank you ... really? When? Would it be possible for us to dine together? Good ... I'll book a table. Ring me when you get back.' A silence, then he laughed softly. 'Indeed, yes ... I'll look forward to seeing you.' He put the telephone down and raised his black head.

'Where were we?'

'The Rassell group,' said Laura.

'Ah, yes,' he said, nodding. 'They're large enough to be of interest to us, small enough to be swallowed ... at present we're proceeding with caution, however.'

'Do they know we're interested?'

He shook his head. 'At present our plans are purely cerebral. We're waiting for a full analysis of their position before we close in on them.'

The smile disturbed her with its connotations of stalking and trapping. She looked at his cold, handsome face and hated him. Aloud, she said, 'Marcus is in favour, though?' Because she wanted to know at all points how far Marcus was behind him and how far he was acting on his own.

Dan read her mind. His dry smile told her as much. 'Marcus is in favour,' he said, then, mockingly, 'Ask him ... if you're ever in any doubt, do ask him.'

'Oh, I shall,' she said, and it was more than a promise, it was a threat.

His smile deepened. 'I'm sure you will,' he drawled, and his reply mocked her ability to do a thing about him. He glanced at his watch. 'Lunch,' he said. 'May I give you some?'

'No, thank you,' she said politely. 'I have a date.' It was a lie. She had planned to eat sandwiches in a park somewhere, but she had no intention of being lured into a relationship with Dan Harland other than the purely business one they had now.

'Of course,' he said lightly. 'Foolish of me to ask.' He stood up and Laura got herself to her feet, feeling very much aware of his superior height and muscle power, the strength of his lean body as he came round the desk towards her. 'Who is it this time?' he asked. 'Joe Laxey?'

'Joe's in Stockholm,' she said. 'No, it isn't Joe.'

'Don't you ever get the strings tangled?' he asked, baffling her for a moment.

Her puzzled eyes answered for her and his mouth twitched. 'It must take both skill and practice, keeping all those men on leads without getting yourself confused.'

'I cope,' she said, chin lifted, turning away. She opened the door and he leaned there, watching her, his eyes travelling over her slender figure from the smooth glossy black head to the small feet. His eyes lingered on her silk-clad legs appreciatively.

'Thank you for getting rid of the boots,' he said.

Laura let the door slam.

In fact she did lunch with someone, because as she walked down the street she bumped into one of their own employees, a friendly young man from the public relations office whom she had met several times when she worked there before.

'Hi!' he said, grinning. 'How's your father? We're all very sorry about his accident.' It was kind but not strictly truthful as Jimmy was prone to sudden outbursts of prickly touchiness whenever he felt he was not being given his due.

David Rees was pleasant enough, however, and Laura smiled back at him. 'He's getting better every day,' she said. 'And how are you? How's the job? Still enjoying it?'

'Very much,' he said. 'Rumour has it you've started working for the T.R. himself.'

'T.R.?' she enquired, frowning.

He winked. 'Tyrannosaurus Rex,' he grinned. 'Harland's nickname.'

Laura threw back her head, laughing. 'That's good. I like it. Yes, I'm working for him. I started today.'

'Got a lunch date?' he asked very casually, and she shook her head. 'Have lunch with me?' He was slightly flushed as he asked and she was about to shake her head when she saw a familiar lithe figure coming out of the building.

She slid her hand through David's arm. 'I'm starving! Come on!'

He was delighted, his grin from ear to ear. Just once, some years ago, he had tried to date her and she had turned him down lightly. Now he was walking on air, his smile proprietorial.

They lunched in an Indian restaurant in the end since it was close by and David could vouch for the cooking. Laura ate chicken dhansak and mushroom bhagi with poppadums and mango chutney, listening while David talked about a film he had just seen. He was far from boring and she was not sorry she had agreed to eat with him. She smiled at him as they walked back to the office. 'I enjoyed that. Thank you.'

'I suppose you wouldn't care to do a film one night?' he asked.

'Love to,' she said without making a thing of it, and he beamed at her.

'When?'

'I'd have to check my diary,' she told him. 'Give me a ring some time and we'll fix it.' She did not want him to think he was getting any green lights. The occasional meeting was fine, but Laura had a positive phobia about possessive relationships. She liked to be fancy free, not tied down.

When she got back to her own office Dan buzzed for her in a sharp, peremptory way and gave her a frozen glare when she went into his office. 'You're twenty minutes late,' he said. 'You have precisely one hour for lunch, no more. Kindly make sure it doesn't happen again.'

Laura was rigid with temper. Nobody had ever said that to her before. She worked hard, often long after hours, and she did not expect to be treated as though she were a slave tied to the desk by a chain.

'Yes, sir,' she said, and her voice was almost hoarse with temper. She had to force herself to say the words and her eyes were filled with bitter animosity. She could have argued with him that, since she often worked late, she was entitled to take her own time over lunch, but she would not give him the pleasure of slapping her down.

He briskly gave her instructions for the afternoon and as she turned to go asked, 'Enjoy your lunch with young Rees?'

'Very much,' she said, glancing at him over her shoulder, her blue eyes cold.

'He's a nice boy and a good worker,' he went on.

'I don't want him driven out of his mind. Play with bigger toys, Laura.'

She stiffened with affront. 'Who the hell do you think you are?'

'The man in charge of making sure the firm runs smoothly,' he said. 'If you send young Rees crazy his work will suffer. Stick with Joe Laxey. I don't give a damn if he goes berserk.'

'Thanks for the compliment,' she snapped. 'But mind your own business ... if I want to go out with David, I will!'

She marched out of the office and began to work with a set, angry face. The afternoon passed rapidly because she was so furious she barely knew what she was doing. Dan had made her sound like Helen of Troy, and it was not intended for a compliment. He was calling her destructive, shallow, flirtatious.

She wished David would ring so that she could accept a date with him, but he didn't, and she got ready to go home with a face like thunder.

On the road home she suddenly saw the limousine behind her and felt her heart flip over like a landed fish. Where was he going? As if she couldn't guess.

They pulled into the drive in file like a procession and she climbed out of her car and confronted him across it bitterly. 'Dinner again?' she asked through tight lips.

He gave her a long, cool look. 'Yes.'

'How delightful,' she said coldly, and her face and voice made it plain that she would like to ram the meal down his throat.

Marcus was pushing him at her. He was determined to throw her at Dan Harland's black head as if she were a fish thrown to a seal, and she knew with certainty that those predatory white teeth would crush her without mercy. She would be consumed.

Her temper really up now, she dressed for dinner with as much care as if she was going to meet the man she loved. She looked at herself in the mirror and was satisfied with her reflection. She had pulled out all the stops. When she walked into the room Dan was there alone, drinking by the window, staring out at a sudden spring rain which filled the soft dusk with tenderness.

He slowly turned and they looked at each other across the room. Laura did not move as the grey eyes passed over her seductively curved outline and the long, slender legs. He looked back at her face without a glimmer of expression.

'Drink?'

'Thank you,' she said, walking forward.

'Martini?'

'Please.'

He put the glass into her hand and they were standing there close together, staring at each other, when Marcus came into the room. He beamed, delighted. 'Ah, you're both here ... good. How did the first day go, Laura?'

'Ask my boss,' she said tartly.

'Oh, I think I can manage her,' drawled Dan, and she was furious with the wording; she knew it was deliberate and Marcus was looking highly pleased.

Over dinner Dan talked about the Rassell affair and she guessed he did it so that she might see that Marcus agreed with every word he said. She was being shown that he had Marcus sewn up. Her grandfather was totally sold on him. He thought the sun shone out of him.

Marcus deliberately cleared off after dinner again. Laura lay back on the sofa watching Dan pour her a drink, her eyes veiled behind her long lashes. She felt the stirring of a cold desire to see him react to her, to make that granite exterior crack.

When he turned and came back she was smiling at him, her eyes very wide and clear, her mouth softly curved upward. He gave her an odd, appraising look and sat down beside her. She accepted the glass, letting her fingers linger on his hand. 'Tell me about yourself, Dan,' she said, and it was the first time she had used his name; his glance made her aware of that, told her that he was aware of it, too.

'What do you want to know?' he asked, leaning back, his arm moving along the back of the sofa behind her head.

'Where did you work before you joined us?'

He considered her drily. 'You want a career report? Certainly.' He briskly, coolly, gave her the bare details of his life, from a training in accountancy through various firms to the day he joined Belsize & Co. He looked like an accountant, she thought coldly. From what he had told her, he had had a steady, rapid rise and no doubt he deserved it. He was shrewd, clever, far-seeing—she knew that already.

She crossed one leg over the other, feeling his cold eyes watch the movement, linger on the long smooth calf exposed by the movement.

She raised her eyes to his face. 'And what do you do in your leisure hours?' she mocked him. 'You do have leisure hours, I suppose?'

'Any sensible man does,' he said. 'Leisure is as important as work.'

'So what do you do with them?'

'Any number of things,' he answered. 'As I told you, I play squash, fence, ride occasionally, go to the theatre, play gramophone records, read ...'

'Alone?' she asked softly. 'Or accompanied?'

He met her eyes thoughtfully. 'If you're asking if I have women, yes, naturally. I'm thirty-seven, Miss Belsize, not a boy, and I have all the usual appetites.'

Her colour was suddenly mounting at the expression in his eyes and the way he had phrased that answer. She shifted back slightly, taken off balance, and he laughed, as if her reaction amused him.

'Am I too blunt for you? I'm sorry. I thought that was what you wanted to know.' He put out one long cold forefinger and slid it down her bare shoulder, making her skin prickle heatedly under his touch. 'Why do you want to know, I wonder?'

She got up because the proximity of his hard body was making her feel airless, she was smothering.

'Will you excuse me, Mr Harland? I'm tired, I think I'll go to bed.'

'Alone?' he asked softly. 'Or accompanied?'

And the repetition of her own words made her draw a sharp breath, her eyes flaring with fury. 'Goodnight,' she snapped with a bite, walking out, because if she stayed she might slap his face.

She heard his car leave as she was getting into bed and felt herself sigh with sick relief because his presence under the same roof was stultifying. She found it hard to sleep. Just as she slid into a light doze she would awake with a start and she knew it was because each time she was reliving the moment when that cold finger touched her skin and she felt herself in mortal danger, but of what she refused to consider.

Over the next few days she found herself easily slipping into a working routine with him, however. The job was not difficult for an intelligent woman. As Dan had quite accurately told her, it was chiefly a matter of managing people. He left it to her to make polite excuses, to coax difficult people, to charm and cozen and arrange matters. She enjoyed it and she knew she was quite good at it. When he became sure that she could be trusted with it he began to leave her to get on with things without his supervision, and she found his trust in her a pleasant experience.

That he was good at his job she soon discovered from observation. He was quick, shrewd, firm, highly organised. He never accepted less than the best, he could be scathing with failures. He wasted neither words nor time. Laura had to admire his ability even though she detested the man.

The one thing that bothered her was that Marcus was still pushing them together. Dan Harland was doing nothing overtly which she could object to, but Marcus had him there to dinner on every possible excuse. He left them alone together. He praised Dan whenever he could. He watched them eagerly and smiled like a lighthouse.

When David Rees rang her to invite her to see the latest French film to hit the box office, she accepted with relief, glad of an excuse to skip dinner with Dan Harland as a silent third.

She rang Marcus to warn him she would not be home that night, and Marcus was almost shrill in his disapproval. 'I don't think it's a good idea for you to go out with one of our own people,' he said, and she scolded teasingly, 'Don't be a snob, darling.'

'Rees ... Rees ... he's in public relations, isn't he?' Marcus muttered just as the door opened. Dan walked over and laid a file on her desk, looking at her, and she lifted her head and nodded to him without expression, answering Marcus quietly.

'Yes, Marcus ... I must go now. I'll see you tomorrow.'

Marcus spluttered as she hung up, but she calmly put the phone down. Dan pushed his hands into his pockets.

'A date tonight?' he asked.

Laura nodded, lowering her head, the glossy black hair swinging over to hide her face.

'Marcus doesn't approve?'

She fiddled with the edge of the file, her long pink nails scratching at it lightly. 'He seems to have other plans for me,' she said with cool deliberation.

There was a silence. 'Which you don't share?' he asked in a voice quite empty of expression.

She lifted her head. Her eyes met his, neither of them giving away a thing.

'Not on your life,' she muttered through her teeth.

He smiled and her blood ran cold. 'Enjoy your date,' he said, going back into his room, and Laura sat and stared at his closed door with a sensation of total panic because in that smile had been threat, amusement, implacable determination and sheer ruthless force. She could run all she liked, but Dan Harland was behind her every inch of the way.

While she and David ate dinner, talked, smiled

and flirted slightly, her mind was frantically going over those moments earlier. She told herself flatly that she was in no danger, she only had to say no loudly and firmly, and there was nothing either Dan or Marcus could do to make her.

But however often she repeated these comforting thoughts to herself, she could not shake off the sensation of panic she had felt when Dan smiled at her.

She had seen sweeter smiles on the faces of tigers as their keepers flung raw meat into their cage.

If only, she thought, he would actually come out and ask her! He had said nothing at all, though. He came night after night and sat there looking at her with those impassive eyes, and she felt the weight of his will pressing down on her as though it were crushing her, but he had never openly said a word.

She even told herself she was going crazy and imagining the whole thing. Perhaps the idea of a marriage had come into Marcus's head, but that did not mean Dan shared his plans. He had never laid a hand on her. Well, she thought, a finger ... did that count? She shuddered, recalling it. Oh, yes, she thought, it counted. Men had kissed her passionately, held her in their arms, touched her with desire, but none of them had ever made her feel the way that one cold finger had made her feel as it lay so lightly on her skin. It had burned through her body from her head to her toes.

She went cold, then hot as she imagined what would happen to her if Dan Harland ever laid a whole hand on her, if he ever touched her in passion, held her.

If he would only come out with it, ask her. She could refuse point blank and it would all be over.

She would cease to feel that silent, remorseless pursuit behind her, as though she were a runaway slave pursued through midnight swamps.

David was holding her hand as the film drew to its tragic, slow conclusion and she looked at him with hidden amusement, realising that he was on the verge of tears. She had barely noticed what she was watching. She had been absorbed, obsessed with Dan Harland.

Ever since she met him that night in her Geneva flat, she thought, she had been obsessed by him. She began to feel suffocated. As David drove her home she looked at him sideways in assessment. She liked him and she could enjoy his company if only she could rid herself of this permanent black shadow. Everywhere she went she was conscious of Dan Harland's presence, as though he were capable of projecting himself to walk beside her, that cold, implacable will dominating her even when he was absent.

David kissed her goodnight and she kissed him back, then stirred and said sleepily, 'Lovely evening, David ... must go in ... give me a ring some time.'

'Soon,' he said eagerly, and she smiled at him. He really was rather a darling. His eyes were so kind and they always held a smile. Dan Harland's ice-locked eyes never held a smile, except when he was ironic. His smiles were like knives, they tore into one, they were to be avoided at all costs.

On her visit to see Jimmy, he asked her: 'Are you keeping an eye on Harland, baby?'

'Both eyes,' she said crisply. 'Permanently.'

Jimmy looked pleased, smiling at her. 'You don't

trust him, either, then?'

'Like I'd trust a boa-constrictor.'

He laughed at that, relaxing against his pillows, the scarred grey face filling with warmth. 'Don't turn your back on him. Be careful—he's clever as well as ambitious.'

'I know,' she said grimly. Dan Harland was more ambitious than Jimmy knew, but she could not tell him of her suspicions. Jimmy would get upset and she did not want to prejudice his chances of a recovery. He seemed much easier in his mind since she began to work for Dan Harland. She was a spy in the enemy camp. Jimmy no longer felt that he was out of action while his rival gained ground daily. He could relax and leave it to Laura to defend their mutual interests, and, looking at her father with loving but wry comprehension, she knew that that suited Jimmy. He had always preferred to get someone else to do his work for him.

Dan Harland was becoming a fixture at the dinner table and Marcus was growing almost coy in his nightly excuses to leave them alone after the coffee. Desperate, she realised that she had to remove herself from her grandfather's house. That week she went flat-hunting and found a place in Bayswater. When she broke the news to Marcus he was first angry, then pathetic. 'You're going to leave me alone? How can you, Laura? Are you bored with your grandfather? Is that it?'

It was his strongest card and he played it for all it was worth, his eyes moist, his manner gloomy. She hated herself, but she would not budge and Marcus gave her a furious, sulky look.

He went off to his study and she knew as if she

were present that he was ringing Dan Harland.

Whatever Dan said to him, he seemed much more cheerful when she saw him later. No doubt Dan had smiled in that tigerish way of his and brushed aside any of Marcus's expressed worries. Dan was not going to be stopped by this little ploy. Laura still worked with him every day. But at least she had stopped his turning up to dinner three or four times a week.

She moved into her new flat a week later. She had a few personal pieces of furniture to arrange, pictures to hang, ornaments to arrange, then the flat was habitable. She settled down on her first evening with a cosy sensation. She had never had a place of her own before. She had always shared with someone.

The knock at the door made her tense. Dan? She slowly went to open it and looked in surprise at the young man standing outside with a tray. 'Welcome, neighbour,' he said, grinning.

Laura pulled herself together. 'This is very kind,' she said, standing back. 'Won't you come in?'

'Thanks,' he said, moving past. He looked around the room and nodded. 'Very nice,' he commented, putting down the tray. He poured her some of the white wine and handed her a glass. 'Well, here's to your new home! I'm Andrew Jackson.'

'Laura Belsize,' she said, smiling.

They sipped the wine. 'How long have you lived here?' asked Laura. 'Are you from the flat over the landing?'

'Three years, and yes,' he said. 'I'm an interior decorator ... I work for Guzburg et Cie's London office.'

'And I work for my grandfather,' she said. 'Belsize & Co ...'

He frowned, giving him the look of a nervous hamster. 'The hotel people? I thought the name was familiar. That's a business with rich pickings.'

'We aren't bankrupt,' she agreed. He was a very thin young man with wiry brown hair in ruffled spikes, dark eyes and a cheerful smile, his age a few years more than her own, she guessed.

'Please, do sit down,' she invited, and they sat facing each other, in whitewood chairs whose seats were filled with puffy quiltwork cushions.

They talked about Andrew's job, which sounded fascinating, and he told her he thoroughly approved the way she had decorated her flat.

'Cheap and cheerful,' she grimaced.

'Attractive,' he corrected. They drank some more of the wine and she put on a tape of Spanish guitar music, turning it down low so that the rippling sounds merely gave pleasant background to their conversation.

'I once saw some flamenco dancers in Madrid dance to this,' said Andrew, getting up. He demonstrated a few steps and Laura laughed.

There was a knock at the door and she went again to open it. More neighbours? she wondered. This could turn into quite a party.

But it was Dan in a black overcoat with a large flat parcel under one arm. 'A housewarming present,' he said, then glanced past her.

Andrew was pouring more wine, humming, but he turned and looked at them, and did a visible double-take. 'Oh,' he said, flushing. He looked at his wine, shrugged. 'Well, I must be going,' he said, and she quickly said, 'Oh, no, there's no need...'

'I've got work to do,' he said, doggedly. 'Nice to have met you, Laura.'

When he had gone Dan closed the door and moved into the flat. She picked up her wine glass and drank a lot of it far too quickly. Dan hadn't said a word, yet Andrew had run off with his tail between his legs. That called for a stiff drink, and wine was not the answer. Laura wished Andrew had brought a bottle of something stronger. She had never felt the need to drink before, but she was feeling it now.

Dan unwrapped his parcel and it was a picture. Had she been asked to guess his taste she would have said a Pieter Breughel, ice-locked lake, wintry landscapes, or a Dutch interior, prim, stiff, formal. She looked at the painting of a single red rose with surprise. It was exquisite, delicate, meticulously drawn. She recalled him sketching a rose on his blotter while he was doodling. She wouldn't have called him a flower person, but there you are... people are never predictable, even men like Dan Harland.

'It's beautiful,' she said. 'Is it an original?'

'You could say that,' he said, and she looked at him in sudden shock.

'Did you do it?' She knew the answer before he spoke and his nod and, 'Yes,' did not surprise her.

'I'm all admiration,' she said, sincere, and he frowned, as though she had hit him.

'I'll leave you to decide where you want it hung,' he said curtly. 'If you want it, that is.'

She was horrified by her own rudeness. It had been a kind gesture. He could have bought her something. He had given her a picture he had painted himself and that made it a far more personal, private gesture. She should have been more grateful.

'Will you have a glass of wine?' she asked, indicating the bottle Andrew had left. He had presumably intended her to finish it.

'No, thank you,' said Dan, looking at it with distaste. He eyed the label as though suspecting poison.

'Coffee?' she asked.

'No, thank you,' he said. 'I've a dinner date.' He walked to the door and she followed, furious to find herself wanting to know who he was dining with—as if it mattered! 'I hope you settle in well,' he said, glancing at the wine again. 'You seem to have got off to a good start. Fellow tenant, was he?'

'Yes,' she said.

He gave her a brief, wry glance. 'Irresistible little creature, aren't you?' Then he went out and the door closed with a quiet click. Laura stared at it for a long time without moving.

## CHAPTER FOUR

IT was from that night that the pattern began to crystallise, that she saw clearly what Dan Harland was doing to her, could do. It began with David. She fell into the habit of spending her week-ends with Marcus because it was one way of silencing his mournful complaints about her flat, and in the warm summer weather which had begun it was pleasant to be at his house. London was fine, but no place to be in the summer heat. She drove down every Friday night and stayed until Sunday night. Sometimes Dan turned up, but she was able to avoid him during the daytime. She kept busy. There was a rough grass tennis court at the side of the house and she and David played tennis there for hours, knocking the balls to and fro casually, neither of them very expert, but enjoying it.

One Saturday she beat David hollow, dancing around the court like a swallow in flight, her slender body graceful as she smashed the ball back to him. When she won she vaulted over the sagging net, grinning at him, and he kissed her. Flushed and laughing, she came from his arms and turned to find Dan watching them.

The pang of alarm which shot through her was like the emotion one might feel confronting an adversary when one was unarmed. She was off balance, shocked.

David was totally unaware, talking cheerfully, as they walked into the house. Dan stood there casually, lean and powerful in a black rollneck sweater and black jeans. He had been riding. He had invited Laura to join him, but she had refused, and he had seemed totally unconcerned. But now his grey eyes were dagger-sharp. David looked surprised when he saw him, although he knew by now that Dan was a frequent visitor to Marcus's house. He gave him a polite, respectful glance, the look an employee gives his boss, and said, 'Hello, Mr Harland ... nice afternoon, isn't it?'

'Delightful,' Dan Harland agreed, but he was not looking at David, his eyes were on Laura's slender figure, travelling slowly and with purpose over the sleeveless, brief tennis dress which revealed quite a bit of her body, his eyes lingering on the long, smooth brown legs.

She felt heat in her veins, an unspecified excitement, and was angry with herself as well as with him.

David took her off to have tea at a pretty tea garden in the next village. There were streams of cars heading for it and it was crowded. David suggested skipping the whole thing, but Laura insisted. She wanted to stay away from the house while Dan Harland was there. After having tea she spent the evening with David and came home very late. Marcus was waspishly irritable. 'Dan was offended,' he told her. 'He is a guest, Laura. You had no business going off like that.'

She carefully said nothing and that maddened Marcus, too. He was torn between a discreet desire to say nothing and a need to make her do as he wished. Unlike Dan Harland, Marcus was in a hurry. He wanted to finalise the whole thing and he couldn't hide that from her. He lacked Dan Harland's icy calm.

It was the following Tuesday that David came to her, hot-cheeked with excitement, his eyes shining. 'They're sending me to Tokyo!' He took her hands and crushed them, beaming. 'For a year! Isn't it fantastic?'

Laura felt herself go cold. David was quite unsuspecting. He was being given promotion, a chance in a million, sent off to Tokyo to master-mind the public relations department over there. They were just branching out in Japan, breaking into a new market. David had a chance to prove himself.

She smiled and congratulated him. David was doing well out of it, anyway. He wouldn't suffer. Dan Harland was being generous.

When she saw Dan next she looked at him through veiled eyes, coldly assessing his menace in a new way, because she had not expected him to go so far. He had removed David from his path easily, though, with the minimum of effort, and it alarmed her.

He did not mention David's new job and neither did she. She was outwardly calm, unworried, doing her work with efficiency. That evening she rang Joe Laxey and he sounded surprised but not displeased to hear from her. She would have liked to confide in him, but it was all so vague and insubstantial. Joe might think she was letting her imagination get the better of her. He might laugh at her. She wished she could laugh at herself.

She had him to dinner in her flat and they talked about Switzerland and Renata and books. They were old friends, and talk was easy with them. When Joe was going, he asked, 'How about seeing the new production of *Camille* with me?' And she smiled. 'Lovely!' Joe grinned. 'Bring two handkerchiefs,' he said, leaving.

Dan eyed her smart black dress with lifted brows. 'Who is it this time?'

'Joe,' she said, unable to repress the faint note of triumph in her voice, because there was no way he could get at Joe Laxey. He did not work for them, he was a wealthy man. Dan would be powerless to stop her seeing Joe.

The grey eyes narrowed on her face as though he could read her thoughts. The smile she feared touched that hard, cold mouth. 'Ah,' he said, and she shivered. Then without another word he walked back into his own office and she sat there trembling as though he had made some appalling threat. Her imagination was getting out of hand, she told herself. Just because Dan had managed to get David Rees transferred out of her life it did not mean that he would try to interfere with every man she saw. She was letting this thing get out of proportion. She had to pull herself together.

Over the next few weeks she saw Joe a number of times, although there was no more to their relationship than there had ever been. They made good companions; they shared a number of tastes; they had mutual friends. And there it stopped—because whatever it was that made the heart beat faster and the blood circulate violently did not happen between them. The friendship was platonic.

During that time Dan Harland's secretary married and left the firm. Her replacement was a svelte blonde with great blue eyes and a breathless way of talking which made her sound oddly naïve, although Laura suspected that to be far from the truth. Olivia Hamilton was far too highly qualified, far too intelligent, for that soft, quick voice to be a true reflection of her character.

Walking into his office after a hurried knock one afternoon, Laura found him at his desk with Olivia's blonde head close to his in an intimate discussion of some letter. The round blue eyes swivelled to the door and Olivia slowly moved away while Dan surveyed Laura coolly. 'Yes?'

She relayed her message expressionlessly before leaving the room. He had told her once that he had women. Was Olivia now one of them? She bent her head over her work, her stomach clenching oddly at the thought of him making love to someone. She could not imagine him losing his head or even losing his control, but she could imagine that he made love as fiercely and powerfully as he played squash, using that finely tuned body of his as if it were an instrument. In her brief glance across his office she had seen Olivia's breast brushing against his arm, and the intimacy of their touching bodies had sent a needle through her. She frowned over her own reactions. Was she jealous? Colour burnt in her face and she shuddered with distaste. God, no, she thought. Even the mere prospect of being touched by Dan Harland made her blood turn to ice.

Dining with Joe some nights later she suddenly caught sight of Dan with Olivia Hamilton on the other side of the restaurant, smiling at each other across their table. The candlelight flickered over Dan's face, giving it black hollows and fierce angles, making it barbaric, the eyes gleaming like steel. Olivia was staring at him with a rapt expression, hanging on to his words.

Laura looked down at her coffee cup. Joe was talking and she laughed when she heard him laugh, but never heard a word he said.

Apparently Joe had been too difficult for Dan to manipulate or remove. He had ceased his pursuit. She could sense it. She felt chill as if she were about to come down with a fever and although she told herself how relieved she was, she felt sick.

Dan Harland had never cared a straw for her, only for the power he would inherit with her, yet the silent duel between them had become a necessity to her. She had found it more and more absorbing, an intense, exciting experience. She felt frustrated, baulked, deprived.

There was a tiny handkerchief of a floor, the golden polished boards set apart from the rest of the restaurant. Joe suggested dancing and they moved out on to the floor. She circled in his arms, then saw Dan with Olivia Hamilton dancing close by. Over Joe's shoulder her eyes met Dan's and her pulses thudded abruptly like the brakes of an underground train in a long tunnel. She almost felt the jerk physically. She stared and could not stop staring. He held her eyes as if by hypnosis.

He looked away first, and spoke to Olivia, who smiled at him. Laura stared at Joe's ear after that and when he spoke to her she jumped.

Joe was amused. 'What's the brown study in aid of?' he asked, and she lied smoothly:

'Tired, I suppose ... sorry, Joe.'

He took the hint, obligingly, and whisked her off home. For the first time that night she dreamed in a heavy sleep and her dreams were all of flight, of fear and panic. She could not see who was following her, but she could hear their soft, secretive steps and she was screaming, a long, voiceless scream she could not make audible.

The following day Dan asked her: 'Your passport up to date still?'

'Yes,' she said, surprised.

'I've got to go to Athens. Want to come?' He did

not make it a request or an order, merely a question, and she hesitated before saying slowly, 'Why not?'

After she had said it she felt that panic coming up in her again and wondered if she were insane to have said she would go. The last person in the world she wanted to fly off with on such a trip was Dan Harland, yet she had agreed to go and now she could not get out of it.

Marcus was delighted. 'I'll visit Jimmy regularly while you are away,' he promised. 'Don't worry about him.'

It was not Jimmy she was worrying about. It was herself. They would be away for five days, which was hardly a lifetime, but in Dan Harland's company it would seem like that.

The day they left she came into the office to find him ready to go, his case packed, his desk clear. 'Oh, by the way,' he said casually, 'Laxey rang for you five minutes ago. I told him you'd be away for the next week.'

She looked at the telephone. 'Maybe I'd better ring him.'

'I shouldn't bother,' said Dan without emphasis. 'He was on his way to an appointment. You'll see him when you get back.'

Their taxi arrived a moment or two later and Laura got into it without thinking any more about Joe, which was a mistake, as she saw later. She should have known. Instinct should have warned her, especially after what happened with David Rees. But her anxiety over the Athens trip had been too much uppermost in her mind. She put Joe aside and forgot him.

Of course, they stayed in one of their own hotels. They were given two-roomed suites on the executive floor, side by side, their balconies communicating. The hotel lay just outside Athens, on the tourist coast, set among palm trees and immaculately maintained flower beds. The white rocks and blue sea made a picture-postcard view from the balconies.

Laura changed into a lightweight blue uncrushable dress and stood on the white-railed balcony staring down over the garden. It was the late afternoon. The smouldering heat of the Greek siesta period lay over the whole hotel. Blinds were drawn, giving the rooms a pretence of coolness. The heat struck up from the asphalt drive like knives.

The hotel garden led across a sandy track to the private beach. She watched the waves cream up on to the sands and saw a few daring souls on lilos with sunhats shading their heads. Along the whitewashed wall ran a creeper thick with bright blue trumpets of flowers she could not put a name to, their colour almost the same shade as the sky.

Dan told her to rest. She went back into her room, found a paperback and lay on her bed reading until her eyes closed and she fell asleep.

They dined at the hotel, taking their time, and Dan talked about the business they had come to complete. 'It will be good experience for you,' he told her, 'watching a deal put through.'

It would be instructive, she thought, watching Dan Harland at work. She had seen one side of him in the office, but now she would actually watch him on the battlefront and it would be a chastening lesson—she was sure of that. Was it what he had brought her here to learn? Was this supposed to make her think twice about resisting his will?

The man they were dealing with was a smooth, sallow-skinned Greek with a charming smile. Laura liked him. He was clever and shrewd, but within hours she knew he was no match for Dan. Dan ran rings around him. She sat there and watched and listened and she saw that Dan was even more formidable as an opponent than she had suspected. Cold, courteous, implacable, he defeated the Greek without ever needing to exert himself an inch. The Greek dealt from behind that charming mask, smiling all the time. Dan was sheathed in stony authority. He would not budge from the position he had taken up and in time the other man conceded to him.

It was an end Laura had foreseen from their first meeting, and she shivered as she admitted it to herself.

Their business was completed in three days; Dan had set himself five. It might have been genuine oversight, but she fancied he had fully intended to have several clear days while they were in Greece.

'Do you know Greece?' he asked, and she shook her head, although he must be well aware that she had not been anywhere but Athens.

'Why don't we drive through the Peloponnese?' he suggested. 'Anyone visiting Greece for the first time should see Corinth, Mycenae ...'

'You know it quite well?' She gave him a mocking little smile.

The grey eyes were half-veiled by those heavy lids. 'I do, as a matter of fact,' he said, and there was a deliberately self-mocking intonation, as though he invited her to smile. 'Greece is the cradle of Western civilisation. Everyone should get to know it. I envy you having all of Greece to discover ... you'll fall in love with it.'

'If you say so,' she said tartly.

'Then you'll put yourself in my hands?' The question was spoken softly and a shiver ran down her back at the image it brought. She lifted her wide blue eyes to him briefly, then looked away.

'As you know Greece I'll be guided by you.' The reply was carefully evasive, but he smiled.

'Good. We'll start early ... I'll hire a car. It will give us the chance to range at will.'

They started in the late dawn when the sun was not yet fully up and the blue shadows crept along sandy roads, the air breatheable and cool. Dan drove as expertly as he did everything else. The open windows sent air rushing over his black hair, ruffling it, lifting his shirt in a balloonlike movement. He had left the collar open and wore no tie. His strong throat was dark brown against the white material.

She sat beside him staring out at the dusty, rocky landscape. The hills beyond Athens were purple-hazed at the crest, home of the famous Hyblos bees which produced the delicious honey she had just eaten for breakfast. 'There's a monastery up there,' Dan told her. 'If we had time I'd take you up to see it. The walls are enormously thick to shut out the glare of the sun.'

'How do you know Greece so well?' she asked.

'I've spent several summers here,' he explained. 'When I was a student I worked on a couple of digs. I once thought I might be an archaeologist, but I changed my mind.'

She frowned, wrinkling her nose. 'I would have

thought it would be preferable to accountancy.'

They took a broad, modern highway on either side of which lay a desert of unfinished buildings, wire fences and modern factories, the ancient landscape scarred by the windblown debris of the twentieth century.

'This was the sacred way to Eleusis,' Dan said in a dry tone, looking out at the factories. 'Worshippers walked along here to take part in the Eleusinian mysteries.'

'What was mysterious about them?' she asked flippantly, and he gave her a faint smile.

'Eleusis was the centre of the fertility cult. Didn't you know? Demeter was the mother goddess of the Greek religion. She was believed to have taught them how to make bread. One of her symbols is the ear of barley.'

'Is there a temple?'

'There was,' he said. 'Now Eleusis is a suburb of Athens, the industrial outpost of the city.'

They drove on to Megara, behind which lay the mountains, their blue shadows lying over the town. 'Once they were full of cranes,' said Dan, lifting his eyes to them.

'Have the cranes all gone now?'

'Unfortunately, yes,' he said, taking the road beside the Corinth canal. He drew up beside it and made her stand on the edge looking down the steep sides to the sparkle of bright blue water, then they drove into the mountains with the sun now rising high in the sky, a tender haze drifting like smoke between them and the island of Aegina which swam in a veil of light in the middle of the jewel-bright sea.

The high wooded road ran through the mountains with the sea on their left, far below, and twisted pines climbed tortuously against the blue sky, the stony ground beneath them thick with their needles. High up on the thyme-sweet slopes she caught a glimpse of shepherd boys with a flock of sheep, the sound of the belled necks ringing out as the animals meandered along. It was not yet hot, but the sky was a cloudless blue. The shadows of the pines made thick bars of black across their road and the light from the sea gave an incredible clarity to everything she saw.

Dan pulled the car into a rough layby and glanced at her. 'Want to look at the sea?' He pulled his door open without waiting for a reply and she followed suit, walking after him to the cliff edge, her breath catching at the fantastic brilliance of blue water. Light danced and dazzled along the waves, striking up at her, and she turned, laughing, to look at Dan.

Sun-blind, her eyes searched for his through a faint haze, and suddenly focused to find him staring at her intently. A strange dizziness swept over her. He bent his head very slowly and she could not move away.

The hard cold mouth touched her lips and a shudder of responsive heat ran through her. His hands caught her shoulders and pulled her against his body, holding her, while his mouth clamped down, opening her lips, leaving her blind and helpless. She had known for a long time that if he ever made love to her she would go crazy, and now under the hot, fierce exploration of his mouth she was unable to think, clinging to him, kissing him back, while his hands pressed her closer and closer until there was not an inch between their bodies.

A car drove past, hooting derisively, and she broke away from him, her face burning. She almost ran back to the car and Dan followed after a moment, climbing into his seat and starting the car without a word. Laura stared fixedly out of the window, trembling, concentrating for dear life on the scenery, making herself take note of the rough heath which was trying to gain a foothold on this stony soil. The summer sun burnt up everything which grew here. Only in the shade of the olive trees and laurels did a few plants manage to find shelter. The landscape reminded her of Dan: the stark, powerful rocky hillsides had his elemental nature. She had feared for weeks that sooner or later he would touch her and she would be helpless to resist him, and it had happened just as she feared. She had made no protest, no attempt to evade. He had taken those kisses as of right and she had slavishly given what he demanded.

'Epidaurus,' he said coolly without looking at her, and she stared around as they drove into the car park. It was already half full and there were tourists everywhere, consulting guide books, talking, their voices echoing in the mountain air.

'This is the Harley Street of ancient Greece,' Dan told her. 'Asklepois was the god of the medical profession, his temple was a hospital, although there was as much superstition as medicine about the way the sick were treated. The theatre is one of the best preserved in the Greek world.'

They began to walk along the sandy track below a belt of pine trees which whispered in a slight breeze. The chirp of cicadas went on among the trees, making the typical sleepy background music of Greece.

'For someone so keen on archaeology I'm surprised you gave it up to be an accountant,' Laura commented in a tight little voice. 'Ambitious to rise in the world, were you?'

He gave her a mocking smile in reply, untouched by her sardonic expression. 'Exactly,' he agreed.

The open air theatre stood below a pine-thick slope, the stone seats rising in a semi-circle. 'If you stand in the top line of seats you can hear what is whispered in the stage,' Dan said. 'They have a peculiar acoustic effect—no doubt that's why the theatre was built here.'

She nodded, but he pushed her slightly. 'Go up and listen,' he ordered.

She reluctantly climbed with a host of other tourists. A guide was giving them a running commentary as he accompanied them, explaining that many votive offerings had been found here. The sick had been expected to give freely to the priests if they wanted Asklepios to help them.

'In the sacred hills behind here was the grove of Apollo,' the guide intoned. 'In these hills the god hunted.'

The tourists all turned to stare at the green shade of the pines and Laura turned, too, but suddenly heard her own name whispered very softly, as if carried on the wind. The hair on the back of her neck bristled and she swung to look down at the stage far below. Dan stood there, his hands dug deep into his pockets, his eyes on her. Her name came again, spoken in a tone which made her shudder. There was cool determination in it, that threat, that will to triumph, which had made her shiver so many times before. His smile had told her all this on other occasions. Now his voice said it. Yes, his voice said. You will do whatever I want. Silently she stared down at his black head, the lean, strong figure, and she felt like a hunted deer.

She hurriedly made her way down to him again and as she joined him their eyes met, but there was no clue in his hard face. Behind those steely grey eyes no flicker of emotion moved, yet she could feel the secret movements of his brain somewhere behind those eyes and she was petrified.

'We'll have lunch at Mycenae,' he said, turning to walk back along the sandy track. 'Do you want to look at the museum here?'

'Why not?' she asked huskily. They spent a quarter of an hour wandering around the little museum, looking at the broken stone figures presented long ago to the god, then they went out once more into the blinding heat of the day. It was noon now and the sun burnt fiercely on their heads as they walked past the whispering, shady pines to the car park. Doves murmured sleepily among the trees, the cicadas made that ceaseless noise, like the ripple of a stream in the distance.

Mycenae's modern village lies in the flat plain below the acropolis. The tiny white houses lay among olive groves and barley fields and Dan drove past them slowly, pulling up outside a small taverna. The owner came out, wiping his oily hands on his apron, the endless wail of bouzouki music coming from inside the cool little room behind him. Dan spoke to him in Greek and the man answered, grinning, coming up to embrace Dan with warmth, touching first one cheek then another to his own.

Astonished, Laura realised they knew each other, and then that Dan, secretive as ever, spoke fluent Greek. Dan turned to take her elbow. 'Ionas, this is Laura,' he said, and the young man smiled at her, shaking her hand.

'Please to sit,' he said in accented English. 'I bring you the best I have, Dan.'

'And that will be the best food you've eaten in Greece, Laura,' Dan said, smiling, and the other laughed, pleased, before rushing back into the restaurant. Dan pulled out a chair and she sat down beside the tiny table. A red-checked tablecloth covered it. Along the trellis above them, shading them, ran a thick tangle of vines, heavy with grapes. A squawking crowd of tiny brown speckled bantam hens ran out suddenly and Ionas chased them away, clapping his hands, grinning at Dan with cheerful black eyes.

'Why didn't you speak Greek to Petrassis?' she asked Dan. During all the discussions with their Athens contact Dan had stuck to English.

He gave her a cool, unrevealing glance. 'It never does to show all one's cards,' he told her. 'I held that one in reserve.'

Laura was icy cold. How many other weapons did he conceal? The little incident seemed to reveal a great deal to her of the convolutions of Dan's thinking. He was a poker player, she thought. There was no way of reading his mind from watching his face.

He watched her and she looked away, bitterly wishing she had the ability to disguise her own mind from him, but afraid that he had already pierced the shell of her mind and knew everything there was to know about her. It was galling to be so obvious.

She remembered the night she had come back to her Geneva flat and stood, transfixed, in the light, blinded by it, unable to see more of him than a dark shape. She seemed to have been struggling ever since to escape from the searchlight he had turned upon her. He was a dark shape even now, watching her from hiding, pursuing her relentlessly.

Ionas came bustling back with a bottle of ice-cold Retsina, two glasses and a dish of fetta cheese and salad. He wished them 'Good eating' in his thick English, smiled and left them to linger over their first course. The cheese had a strong taste, but with the wine it was delicious. While Laura sipped from her glass, Dan leaned over suddenly and flicked an insect from her throat and the brief touch of his fingers made her quiver. The grey eyes saw the slow recoil and narrowed, but he said nothing.

The food, as Dan had promised, was delicious. Ionas had pulled out all the stops. The smoky lamb, cooked over charcoal and spiked with rosemary, was so tender it seemed to melt in her mouth.

After they had finished their meal they sat in the vine-rich shade in the heat of the afternoon, occasionally picking a grape and eating it, drinking thick, sweet coffee, talking lazily. Laura felt sleepy, lethargic, filled with disinclination to move. She leaned back against one of the wooden posts supporting the trellis, listening while Dan talked about Greek history.

'You love this country,' she said.

His smile was filled with charm which seemed to knock the breath from her body. 'Yes,' he said.

She had never seen that charm before. He kept it hidden, and perhaps, she thought, it was one of those concealed weapons of his, only used when he judged it suitable. It was a potent weapon, anyway. The cold contours of his face were illuminated by it, as though his features were stony hillsides lit with sudden sunshine.

Ionas came out and sat beside Dan, talking to him in guttural English, smiling at them both. Laura discovered that Dan had worked here in Mycenae some years ago, that he had visited the place often since. 'We once fought over a girl,' Ionas told her, grinning, and at Laura's look of amazement, laughed out loud. 'It is true. No, Dan?'

Dan stared at Laura with a slight smile hovering around his well-cut mouth.

'You don't ask who won,' Ionas said slyly.

She glanced at him, smiling. 'Oh, I'm sure you did.' In fact she was sure of the opposite, but she said it to annoy Dan.

He laughed softly, however, quite untouched. Ionas roared and slapped his thigh. 'She teases you, I think, Dan.'

Laura lifted her eyes to meet Dan's mocking eyes. 'She always does,' he murmured, a taunt in his tone.

Some other customers arrived at that moment and Ionas excused himself. Laura nervously looked at her watch. 'Shouldn't we be getting on?'

Dan shrugged. 'Is there any hurry?' But he got up, said a few more words to Ionas and they drove away, while Ionas waved and smiled.

'Who was the girl you fought over?' she asked.

He gave her a little smile. 'I thought you were indifferent,' he said.

She flushed. 'What do you mean?'

'You showed no interest when Ionas spoke of her.'

She shrugged. 'I just wondered.'

He stared at the narrow, dusty road. 'I forget her name. She was a pretty creature, though.'

'Greek?'

'Yes, as dark as you are,' he said, still watching the road. 'But her skin was olive and her eyes black.'

She wondered if the girl had loved him, whether he had been her lover, and felt that now familiar flick of burning excitement at the idea of Dan making love. She closed her eyes, biting her lower lip. He was invading every corner of her mind, as insidious as a snake, a cold, smooth enemy penetrating her and possessing her. Her lids flicked open in abrupt fear, as though she felt his hands on her, and he was watching her, his dark head turned towards her, his eyes narrowed.

She looked away, shivering. 'You might at least have remembered her name,' she said.

'Why should that worry you?' he asked, still watching her.

'You make it all so impersonal,' she said tightly. 'Did you make love to her?'

'Do you sleep with Joe Laxey?' he asked, and the question took her totally by surprise, her face flushing, her eyes flying to his face.

'What?' Her voice was shaking.

'If we're to exchange romantic confidences let's be equal,' he said. 'You've been going around with him for years, according to Marcus. There has to be more to it than your usual little flings.'

'What do you think you know about it?' She was scornful, angry that Marcus should have told him anything about her.

'I've seen you walk out of a man's arms with

amusement after he's gone wild over you, remember,' he said, and she was baffled for a moment, staring at him.

'What are you talking about?'

'The fellow in Geneva,' he said. 'The unhappy Max ... whom you handed over to your flatmate with such calm unconcern, as though he were a doll you no longer wanted.'

She gave him a hard stare. 'I'm very fond of Max, as it happens.'

He laughed, his mouth hard with sardonic amusement. 'Never be fond of me, sweetheart. I might get very nasty.'

Her colour burned. 'I'd see you in hell first!'

His mouth curled. 'Would you?' he said oddly, turning to watch the road. 'Would you, indeed, Laura?'

'Marcus has no right to talk to you about my private life,' she snapped, unsure about the thought behind what he had said.

'Ah, yes,' he murmured. 'Marcus has those plans for you ... the ones you object to.'

She sat erect, stiff, waiting for him to go on, wondering if he was about to propose to her at last, and nerving herself for a refusal.

'You haven't told me yet,' he said, instead.

She frowned. 'Told you what?'

'Is Laxey your lover?'

A denial was on her lips when she drew it back, her face confused. 'That's my business,' she said flatly.

'You asked me first,' he shrugged. 'Why should I be expected to answer questions if you won't?'

Angrily she said, 'I don't give a damn whether you

slept with your Greek girl-friend or not.' And she knew she lied. She cared, and she was bitterly angry with herself for caring.

'No?' He was smiling again, staring at the road. 'But I care. After that very promising exchange on the road above the sea it would be interesting to know.'

She drew in a furious breath. 'Go to hell!'

He laughed, turning to look at her with eyes filled with mockery. 'Now I wonder why that makes you look so desperate?' he asked in a teasing voice, and that charm was back, it filled his eyes and made his mouth warm.

They were climbing the hills to the old citadel which stared down over the plains, with the heathery purple in the background, reminding Laura vaguely of Scotland, except that the dry summer grass, bleached almost white by the sun, bore witness to this fiercer climate.

The path from where they parked the car ran over stony, dusty ground to the square, lintelled gate. They paused before it, staring up at the great triangular lintel carved from limestone bearing two heraldic lions on each side of a column. It was familiar—she had seen it many times in illustration. Yet, seen with her own eyes, it was strange and awe-inspiring. Through that gateway lay one of the world's most famous cities in ruins.

Names seemed to fill her deafened ears ... Agamemnon, Orestes, Clytemnestra ... on these walls sentries had stalked the night by torches, watching the plains for enemies, and within them the passions and hatreds of long-dead men had flared and devoured. Dreamily she turned and found Dan watching her in silence.

'I'm almost afraid to go in,' she said. 'It seems sacrilegious.'

'Don't tell me you're romantic,' he mocked, and she flushed.

'I won't.'

He curved a hand around her wrist and pulled. 'Come on.' As they walked through the gate he pointed to a small, square opening in the inner wall. 'That was the gatehouse. The guards sat in there when it was raining.'

A cold, grim little room, she thought, peering at the tiny cave-like room, imagining a shivering soldier squatting over a smouldering little fire inside it.

They walked over rough uneven ground to the grave circle. A wall of stones fenced in the burial places. Dusty, stark and empty, they lay below her feet. Once the high dead of the city had lain there. 'Mycenae, rich in gold,' Dan murmured in her ear. 'And empty of it now ... except the gold they take from the tourists who stare into the gutted graves.'

Laura stood with him by the citadel walls staring down into the sun-dazzled plain, the colours all melting into each other, dusty green and white and grey, each shade almost fractionally different, yet from this height all taking one uniform tone.

'Perhaps on summer evenings Clytemnestra stood here,' Dan said dryly, 'plotting the murder of her husband.'

'He deserved it for killing her daughter,' she retorted.

'Women's Lib rearing its ugly head?' he mocked.

'Common decency,' she said. 'I never cared much

for Agamemnon ... a self-willed, arrogant man.'

His eyes met hers and he grinned. 'Do I detect a meaning behind that?'

'Arrogant, ambitious men usually get their comeuppance,' she said, turning away.

He followed her over the stony ground. 'And usually at the hands of an even more ruthless woman,' he suggested.

She did not answer, so he paused before saying coolly, 'Shall we go and see the tholos before we leave?'

'Why not?' she asked, turning down the hill. The tholos, or beehive tomb, lay below the citadel, stone-built, on the beehive pattern, rising to a curved tapered point in the centre. At one point in the city's history Mycenae's kings had been buried in them. Laura followed Dan down the shaft into the tomb, a musty odour clinging to the stone walls. In twilight dimness they stood inside, staring up at the way the central stones were fitted together with incredible craft and skill so that not a sliver of wood could be slid between them. The further they moved from the entrance the darker it became until they stood in an inner tomb where the light did not penetrate.

They were alone for a moment in total darkness and silence. Dan breathed softly beside her and she closed her eyes, shivering. He moved behind her, his hands taking her shoulders, pulling her back so that she leaned against him. His fingers moved over the bones of her back, pressing them firmly and gently, then up to her nape, fingering it. Her heart was beating raggedly and she could not move. She felt his breath on her skin, then his mouth moving over her neck. He kissed it softly, brushing it, then with more depth, until his mouth was hot on her shivering throat and she was groaning huskily, unable to stop the broken sounds she was making.

He turned her into his arms fully and his mouth came down to meet hers as it lifted hungrily. His arms tightened as she came alive under his kiss and she wound her arms round his throat, her blood racing along her veins.

The flare of a match made them jump apart. In the dim light a man stared at them, grinned and said something in Greek. She ran out of the entry and Dan followed. In the sloping shaft he caught up with her, taking her arm. She wrenched it away from him.

'Keep your hands off me!'

'That's a change of tune!' he said with a taunting smile.

Her face was burning hot. 'Just stay away from me!'

In silence they reached the car and he drove away, but sitting there with fixed blind eyes Laura was inwardly shaking, her skin bearing the imprint of his hands wherever they had touched her, as though his fingermarks were brands stamping him her master. He could no longer be in any doubt that she was vulnerable to him. She had given herself away too fully.

She did not say a word as they drove back towards Athens and she did not look at him once, yet all the time she was deeply, violently aware of the poised, lithe body seated so casually beside her, his sun-browned skin firm over his muscled flesh. That tan looked good under the cap of his thick black hair, and the hard, handsome features had been drawing female attention everywhere they went that day. She had seen the way women looked at him and been flicked with jealousy, furious with herself. The coldness in the grey eyes merely enhanced his good looks, adding to the allure he exuded.

It made women speculate upon their chances of breaking through that ice, lighting the grey eyes.

She looked at her hands. Not me, she thought. I'm not getting caught in that trap.

On their last day in Athens she was tired, the long car journey and the heat and dust of the day making her drawn. She spent the morning lounging on the beach in the shade of a large canopy and swam before lunch to give herself an appetite she lacked. Dan came down to the pool having spent the morning on the telephone, it seemed, doing business with Greek contacts in the city. Laura was pacing herself down the blue water of the pool when he hit it beside her and she started in surprise. The brown chest rose, dripping, from the bottom and he shook back his black hair, staring at her.

She felt a flickering panic at the sight of his bare shoulders and turned, swimming away. He followed and it became a race, a race she had no more hope of winning than she had won their game of squash. He could outdistance, outswim her every time, but he chose to keep stroke with her, turning the strong cold face towards her, staring at her.

She moved to the steps to leave the pool. Dan emerged beside her and for a few seconds they stood staring at each other. He dropped his eyes over the whole length of her body inch by inch as if he were taking an X-ray picture of her, and she trembled as though each look were a caress, then she ran from him, clenched against the sensations she was prey to, bitterly angry with herself and him.

During lunch she retrieved her self-respect by behaving calmly, even when his hand brushed hers when he poured some wine into her glass.

'What do you want to do for the rest of the day?' he asked, looking coolly at her over the rim of his own glass.

'Shop,' she said. It was the most innocent occupation, she thought. A safe way of passing their final afternoon here.

He nodded. 'Want to buy some souvenirs? The Monastiraki area is the best place in Athens for that. I'll take you there. It's a flea market, full of stalls, you can buy anything from a dagger to a first century curio. You take your chance on whether it's genuine or not, and whether it's stolen or not, too.'

'There's no need for you to come,' she said, not quite meeting his eyes. She desperately wanted to get away from him for a few hours. He was beating down her resistance and she needed to be out of his company.

He laughed softly. 'Ah, but there is,' he said, and his voice left her in no doubt as to his meaning. He knew exactly why she wanted to get away and he had no intention of letting her escape. She looked at him then, eyes wide and frightened, and that charm was in his face again, that teasing, mocking amusement. Dan Harland was turning a blow-torch on her now. He had speeded up his pursuit and the chase was now in desperate earnest. Laura felt her throat closing up and swallowed, lips dry.

## CHAPTER FIVE

On the outskirts of Athens tall, recently built flats dominated the skyline. Outside the shops stood baskets of fruit; melons, with smooth dark green skins, cut in half, their pink flesh running with juice, tomatoes of much larger size than English ones, piles of dark-bloomed grapes and imported peaches. They drove up through the city to the Leoforas Olgas, past the bus terminal, past which Dan pointed, saying, 'There's the Zappeion Park. They have the tallest palm trees I've ever seen ... real giants.' At the top of the hill he turned right past Byron's statue and into Syntagma Square, the heart of Athens, with its tree-shaded cafés. Laura's eyes lingered on the blue sky to the left where the white pillars of the Acropolis cleaved the cloudless horizon. She knew she would never forget that sight, the profile which meant Athens.

The streets were thick with traffic. Taxis darted like hooting minnows through the stream, their drivers leaning out to insult each other with gold-toothed mockery, a sparkle in their eyes. Horns constantly blared. Drivers cursed. There was a daring audacity about the way men drove in the narrow streets.

Dan insisted on having a glass of citrus before leaving Syntagma Square. They sat at one of the closely packed tables under the trees watching the cars. A glass of water automatically appeared alongside their citrus drink. The ice-cold water was ambrosial on this hot afternoon. Greeks revere water. They never take it for granted. It is too precious in their dusty, stony land.

Afterwards they walked through the shopping streets to Monastiraki—a web of crowded alleys spreading from one main street. Beaten metal work, toys, weapons, army uniforms and souvenirs of all sorts could be bought from stall after stall. She bought some gifts for Marcus, Jimmy and Joe Laxey, sent a postcard to Renata in Geneva and, on impulse, another to Max, with Dan's unreadable eyes watching as she wrote a few words on it.

After they had walked across the stony moon landscape of the Agora below the Acropolis, they emerged into the Plaka, the Turkish district of Athens which had once housed Byron, the tall, terraced houses decaying in picturesque but shabby beauty, shutters awry, roofs crumbling, paintwork sun-warped. She was hot and tired now, feet aching, and glad when Dan suggested a drink in one of the many tiny shady tavernas in the area.

They passed the entrances to open courtyards, cobbled and whitewashed, where children's voices echoed in laughter, passed a Greek church shaded by palms and descended the steps into a taverna. After the glare of the sun it was a refreshing change to sit down in the cool dim little room and drink ice-cold citrus and the inevitable glass of water. Laura closed her eyes wearily and almost slid into sleep. The touch of Dan's cool fingers on her cheek woke her and her eyes opened at once, alarmed.

'Shall we have another glass of citrus?' he asked.

While she slept he had moved closer, his knee against her own.

'If you like,' she said huskily.

His eyes moved to her throat where a pulse was throbbing wildly. 'After that I suggest we go and light a candle to St Basil,' he said.

Baffled, she stared at him. His smile was filled with charm.

'Don't you know that if you do that you're sure to come back to Greece?'

'I'm sure I shall anyway,' she said.

'You like Greece, then?'

'Who could dislike it? It's the most fabulous place I've ever seen,' she said frankly.

His eyes were very close and she wondered how she had ever imagined they were icy. They held smiling warmth. Little flecks of blue seemed suddenly to float in the grey, like diffused atoms around the black nucleus of his pupil. Her own eyes gazed into his, a smile hovering around her mouth.

'One day ...' he began, then broke off, and she waited, but he did not continue with whatever he had been about to say.

The waiter brought their drinks and left, giving them a smiling, sly glance. 'You're very flushed,' Dan said smoothly. 'It must be the sun.'

He put a finger against her cheek, stroking the warm curve, and she sighed, half protesting, half submitting to the contact, then she moved back and picked up her glass, drinking the refreshing liquid thirstily.

They walked back to the church and went inside. A few women knelt there, kissing the icons on the wall. Barbaric, glittering, the heads of the saints stared out in that formalised beauty, silver and gold giving them a rich sheen which mitigated the harsh severity of their features. Laura lit a candle and knelt before St Basil while the black-bearded priest stood in the back of the church watching her curiously. The air was thick with incense, the corners black-shadowed. Dan lit a candle and knelt, too, astonishing her. She watched, wondering what he prayed for, not daring to ask.

After leaving the church they walked back up to Ermou Street to buy a final present which Dan had remembered he should get. 'For Olivia,' he said lightly, and she gave him a quick, searching look. He turned his head and met her eyes.

A little quirk lifted his mouth. Suddenly she remembered having heard him talking on the phone one day to someone called Olivia. 'Did you know Olivia before she came to work for you?' she asked him, bluntly, and he grinned.

'How do you know that?'

'I just remembered hearing you talk to her on the phone the first day I worked for you.'

He lifted one eyebrow. 'Did you? Yes, I knew her. She worked for me in a previous job.'

Worked for him, she thought, or slept with him? Her blue eyes darkened and he watched her, his smile curious.

'And now what's going on inside that head of yours?' he asked with a twist of the lips.

'It must be convenient for you,' she said softly. 'Having someone you know so well stepping in to work for you.'

'Very,' he said shortly, but there was a glitter in

the grey eyes now. Her smile and soft tone had annoyed him.

'Does Marcus know that Olivia is ... an old friend?' she asked in a sweet voice.

His brows drew together and he gave her a brief, cold look. 'Not yet, but no doubt you'll make sure he does.'

'Is there any reason why he shouldn't know?' she asked innocently.

'No,' he said tersely.

'But you never mentioned it before? How strangely forgetful, Dan,' she murmured, eyes lowered, smiling.

He halted, looking down at her through narrowed eyes. 'You little bitch,' he muttered, so softly that the words shocked her. She looked up, eyes wide, astonished. It was the first time she had got through that hard outer casing of his and she was both surprised and alarmed by her successful hit, because it had to mean that Olivia was important to him, that he had taken a risk in bringing her into the firm to work for him, that he knew Marcus would disapprove.

'Charming language,' she snapped, walking away. Dan caught up with her and they got back into the car in silence, driving back to their hotel without exchanging another word.

She dressed for dinner with care that evening. Her skin was sunwarmed, a smooth golden brown, since she took the sun easily and quickly, her skin naturally responsive to it. She wore a plain, simple white dress with a halter neckline which left her shoulders bare. When she joined Dan he threw a comprehensive look over her but said nothing. They ate in leisurely silence, but after dinner there was an exhibition of Greek dancing on the minute floor between the tables.

Afterwards the guests were invited to join the dancers. Laura was reluctant, shy at the idea, but Dan dragged her up by the hand. He was, she found, already skilled in the dancing, and the Greeks applauded his lithe movements, grinning at him.

Later the band played Western music and the dancing became the usual variety, some guests dancing close together, others standing apart, not touching.

This was how Laura usually danced and she grinned at Dan as she moved around him, avoiding him. He watched her with those narrowed, glittering eyes for a few moments, his glance moving up and down over her slender figure as she moved, then he put out a hand and jerked her into his arms. As their bodies touched she felt something tighten inside herself. It was almost as though she had been provoking, inviting him to act just as he had, moving out of reach, waiting for him to take her, and now she was satisfied.

'Why haven't you married Laxey?' he asked her suddenly.

She looked up. 'Neither of us wanted to be tied down,' she said lightly. 'We both feel happier in open relationships.'

He was expressionless. 'You prefer to flit from one man to another, do you?'

She smiled. 'That's it.'

'You can't be in love with Laxey, then,' he said.

'Did I ever claim I was?'

'Does he imagine you are?'

'I doubt it.'

'Is he in love with you?'

'You would have to ask him that,' she shrugged.

'What a cold little fish you are,' he said dismissively.

Her colour rose and she was angry. 'It takes one to know one,' she snapped through her teeth.

His eyes flashed down to her face. 'So it does,' he said in a curious voice. 'Have you ever been in love?'

Her colour deepened. 'No,' she said far too quickly.

He considered her with his black head to one side, face unreadable. 'Judging by my own experience of you, you have the usual instincts,' he said as coolly as if he were talking business.

Her face seemed to flame and she would have liked to wrench herself out of his arms, but she made herself go on moving with him, trying hard to look less disturbed.

'No comeback?' he asked softly, probingly.

She met his eyes. 'I enjoy lovemaking,' she said in brittle tones. 'It doesn't mean a thing.'

His face didn't alter by an inch. His eyes went on watching her, his mouth a cool, straight line. 'Which sounds amazingly frank, until you inspect it closely,' he said. 'But I already knew you liked having me make love to you, so you were giving nothing away at all, were you, Laura?'

She gave him a little smile, hoping he could not see her face too clearly in the dim light. 'I never give anything away if I can help it,' she said.

After a silence, he asked, 'What have you got against marriage?'

Her body tensed. 'I get claustrophobic at the

thought of it,' she declared. 'Shades of prison bars.'

He laughed, his face altering. 'Are you kidding?'

Her eyes lifted to his face. 'No,' she said flatly.

His smile faded. He stared at her. 'So ...' he said very softly.

Laura's voice thickened, her body trembled. 'Once you marry you become one man's possession, you lose your own individuality ...' The words to express her views escaped her. She stopped dead, her voice fraught.

'Go on,' Dan said sharply.

She shrugged. 'I can't put it into words.'

'Is it marriage you find so frightening, or love?' he asked, and the question threw her into wary confusion, because it was love, and she knew it, but for some reason she did not want him to know it. Marriage was merely the outward symbol of the possession love could impose. It was the smothering, devouring emotional possession which she feared and had always evaded. She remembered the darkness of the tholos in which she had submitted to his kiss and shivered. In that airless, lightless tomb she had come very close to the heart of the darkness she feared.

The music ended and she broke away quickly, saying, 'I think I'll go to bed now ... goodnight.'

She was in flight and they both knew it. But Dan stood there, watching her almost run to the lift, and he made no attempt to follow her.

Next morning they met at breakfast almost like strangers, pleasantly polite strangers, and drove to the airport in the early morning coolness without exchanging more than an occasional casual glance.

During the flight she pretended to sleep, eyes tightly shut. Dan read some papers, his dark head hidden behind them. They had come to know each other much better during their days in Greece and she suspected he had intended that they should. At least now he knew how strong her dislike of marriage was—perhaps now he would cease his pursuit of her. She had made her inclinations plain.

He drove her down to Marcus's house from the airport, following her into the house after parking the car. Mrs Jacques met them anxiously and at once burst out, 'Oh, miss, I'm glad you're back! He wouldn't let me cable you ...'

Laura's face whitened. 'My father!' she exclaimed, and Dan moved to put an arm around her, supporting her as she swayed.

'No, miss,' said the housekeeper unhappily, looking at Dan. 'It ... it's the master ... he had another attack.'

'Another?' Laura looked at Dan, confused and alarmed. 'What does she mean?'

'Where is he?' Dan asked Mrs Jacques.

'Oh, in his room. We got a nurse. He wouldn't stay in the hospital. He said he was better.' Her eyes were miserable. 'But he isn't. He's so grey.'

'What are you talking about?' asked Laura hoarsely, angry because she had been excluded from some secret known to both of them apparently.

'Would you get us some tea, Mrs Jacques?' Dan asked over her head, then, as she began to protest, guided her into the drawing-room, his arm holding her waist firmly.

He closed the door and she looked at him crossly. 'What's going on? What's wrong with Marcus?'

'His heart,' Dan said briskly. 'He began to have trouble with it a couple of years ago, but he obstinately went on working. When I joined the firm he kept it from me for a few months, then one day he had an attack at the office. I spoke to his doctor and discovered that Marcus shouldn't be working at all ... that was when I took over at the firm and Marcus started staying at home.'

Laura listened, pale and tense. 'Is it bad?'

'Very bad,' he said bluntly. 'And that's why I have to talk to you before you go up to see him.'

'I have more sense than to upset him,' she said indignantly, her eyes angry.

He looked at her almost hesitantly, as though he were searching for words. 'There's more to it than that, Laura.' The door opened behind him and Mrs Jacques wheeled in a tea trolley and began to fuss about with the cups. 'We'll deal with that,' Dan said brusquely, getting up, and the housekeeper looked at them both quickly before going out and closing the door behind her without a sound.

Laura said, 'I'll do it,' and got up to pour the tea. Dan leaned back against the cushions, watching her slender figure as she poured the tea. She handed him his cup, offered him biscuits, to which he shook his head in silence.

When she sat down with her own cup, he watched her with his most unreadable expression, his grey eyes slits between those heavy lids.

'It's time we stopped fencing around,' he said coolly. 'We're both well aware that Marcus is hoping to hear that while we were in Greece I persuaded you to marry me.'

Her cup tilted. Hot-cheeked, she clumsily placed it on the trolley. 'Well, isn't that too bad,' she said in angry, clipped tones.

'Marcus has set his heart on it,' he replied, the hard, handsome face set in its most impenetrable mask.

'No!' she cried hoarsely.

'Your grandfather planned our marriage in order to make sure that the firm would be safe.'

Laura gave him a bitter look. 'I thought he ensured that by leaving you as my trustee!'

He smiled coldly. 'That's temporary. Marcus is still afraid you'll marry someone as useless as your father.'

'He needn't worry. I've more sense than to marry at all,' she said.

His eyes held a peculiar glint. 'So you say now, but women have been known to change their minds.'

'I shan't.'

'Even so,' he said smoothly. 'I'm afraid that the prospect of having you in control of the firm is unlikely to make Marcus rest easier than he does at present. You may have more sense than Jimmy, but you're still a young woman with little management experience.'

She stood up and walked restlessly around the room. 'I love my grandfather, but I'm damned if I'm going to marry a man I dislike merely for the sake of the firm!'

Dan leaned back against the sofa, his black head resting on the cushions, his face inscrutable. 'You're not seeing the problem logically. If, as I suspect, it's love rather than marriage you fear, I don't see that you need to worry. Surely marrying a man you don't love will be safer than marrying one you do?'

She stared at him, confused and bewildered. Her

pulses throbbed, her eyes seemed dimly troubled. 'I ... no, you're ...' She could not frame an answer sensibly enough, her thoughts were too jumbled.

'It would give your grandfather more happiness than you can imagine,' he said softly.

'Do you think I don't know that?' she demanded irritably, glaring at him.

'And you still refuse to give him that relief, that happiness?' He sounded coolly disparaging, and she flushed.

'You make it sound as though I were refusing him a trifle ... we're talking about my life!'

'We're talking about his,' he said quickly. 'He's desperate to see you marry me—you know that.' His eyes narrowed on her. 'You've known it for months, haven't you, Laura?'

Her colour deepened. 'You both made it transparently obvious.'

'And you made your reaction transparently obvious,' he said with a faint hard smile.

'This is the twentieth century, for heaven's sake. Marcus can't arrange my marriage as though I were a child!'

'He's a very sick man and he's very anxious about both your future and the future of the firm,' he told her. 'You'll be a very wealthy young woman one day. Marcus wants to protect you as well as protect the firm.'

She turned and gave him a bitter, cold look. 'And he expects to do that by marrying me off to *you*?'

His glance was level and guarded. 'Yes,' he said softly.

'Well, I won't!'

He stood up and walked towards her and she

backed away like a hunted child, her face shifting with confused emotion. 'Stay away from me!'

'I want your promise to marry me,' he said. 'And I want it now.'

She had backed to the window and stood there, at bay, watching him with wide eyes.

Dan put a hand under her chin, his fingers gripping her calmly, tilted her head so that he could stare down into the wide blue eyes. She tried to pull her head away, her hair brushing over his fingers.

'This is a business arrangement, Laura,' he said, the grey eyes holding hers. 'I know how much you love your grandfather. It will make him very happy and relieve a lot of the pressure which is causing these attacks. Your father has given Marcus a lot of anxiety in past years. It's up to you to redress the harm Jimmy has done.'

'Don't play on my loyalties, you ...'

His fingers shot to her lips, silencing her. He gave her a faint grin. 'Now, now—language! You've made it pretty clear what you think of me. Just look on the whole thing as a business merger. If there was another man it would be different. You say you never mean to marry—well then, what difference will it make? Ours will be a marriage of convenience on both sides.'

Put like that, it sounded rational and comprehensible, but it did not lessen the dark shadow which he had always summoned to oppress her. She gave a furious sigh. 'You've always meant to have your own way!'

He grinned again, that terrible charm in his face, and she felt a smile touching her own face, trying to banish it without success.

'Say yes,' he murmured, bending over her.

'You're maddening,' she muttered, grinding her teeth.

He took her hand and she felt something cold against her skin. Looking down, she saw the blue flash of a sapphire and gasped at the size of it. 'Extravagant of you!' And arrogantly self-confident, she thought. He never doubted he would win.

'Now come and tell Marcus,' he said softly, taking her hand.

As she looked across the elegant, charming bedroom she saw Marcus lying against banked pillows with a pathetically hopeful look on his pale face, and she saw at once that he had waited for them to return because he had hoped that during their trip to Greece Dan would succeed in getting her to marry him.

He looked shrunken and older than ever, his cheeks hollow, his eyes deep sunk. Laura pulled her hand from Dan's controlling fingers and ran to him, tears in her eyes. 'Oh, Marcus ... why didn't you tell me? Why didn't you send for us?'

Marcus was looking at her hand even as she spoke and a blissful smile ran over his face. 'Well, well, what's this?' he asked, pretending bafflement.

Dan had moved to her side and lifted her, an arm around her waist, his hand clamped beneath her breast in a possessive gesture which made her heart thud. 'Laura and I are going to be married,' he said softly.

Marcus sighed and beamed. 'Good heavens,' he said, opening his eyes wide. 'Is it true, Laura?'

She leant over to kiss him on the cheek. 'Yes,' she said, feeling as she spoke that she was burning her bridges with a vengeance. 'Are you pleased?'

Marcus abandoned pretence and his eyes glowed. 'I'm very happy,' he said, then he gave a hand to each of them. 'You couldn't have pleased me more, darling. Dan is a rock.'

How apt, she thought, but she smiled. 'So he is,' she agreed, and Dan gave her a brief, secret, comprehending look, as though he read her hidden rebellion.

'When are you getting married?' Marcus asked, and she opened her lips to reply, but Dan had already answered for both of them.

'As soon as we can,' he said, and she sucked in her breath with dread and dismay because he was going to stampede her now, she could see that. He would give her no time to reconsider, to back out. Now that he had got her to accept him he would not let her go again.

'You look tired, Marcus,' he said, smiling at her grandfather. 'You must rest. Kiss him goodnight, Laura.'

The command infuriated her, but she obediently bent and kissed her grandfather, who smiled at her lovingly. 'Now kiss Dan, darling,' he said in pleading tones. 'I want to see that. I've waited a long time for it.'

Dan drew her towards him before she had time to say a word and bent his head, kissing her warmly, yet oddly impersonally. When she looked at Marcus he was smiling, already looking sleepy.

They went out and she waited until they were alone once more in the drawing-room before declaring, 'I'm not being rushed into marriage!'

'We've no time to waste,' said Dan. 'Don't make

difficulties, Laura. You've accepted the principle of the thing.'

'What principle is that?' she asked bitterly. 'And what would you know about principles?'

His eyes glinted as if he were angry. 'We're both doing this for Marcus.'

She laughed sardonically. 'Oh, are we? I thought you were doing it to get those grasping hands of yours on the firm.'

A faint red ran along his hard cheekbones. His eyes glittered like ice in sunlight. 'As you prefer,' he said, oddly. 'However, since it is to happen, the sooner the better.'

She was suddenly too tired to argue. 'Oh, very well,' she shrugged, 'Can we discuss it tomorrow? I'm tired and I want to get some rest.'

He studied her clinically. 'Yes, you look dead on your feet,' he agreed. 'Very well, I'll drive down tomorrow, then.' He walked to the door, paused. 'By the way, when I spoke to Laxey just before we left I told him you were going to marry me.'

Laura was suffused with angry, burning colour. 'You did what?'

He gave her a dry smile. 'And I don't want you seeing him again. Marcus has old-fashioned ideas about marriage. He wouldn't be happy to know that his granddaughter had extra-marital relationships.'

'Why, you ...' Before the furious words could burst from her Dan had opened the door and walked out, closing it quietly on the insults which tumbled from her.

The cold-blooded, calculated way he had spoken sent blood in waves to her head. He had told Joe before they left for Athens: he had been that sure of her. She should have guessed he was up to something, she thought. She should have known when he mentioned having spoken to Joe, but she had blithely gone off forgetting the whole thing.

She looked back over her long flight from him and knew she had never had a chance of escape. He had known that. He had never hurried because he had never doubted he would get her.

For one moment she contemplated going up to Marcus and telling him she couldn't go through with it. Then she remembered his frailty, his happiness, his relief. She could not do that to him. Marcus relied on Dan Harland now. He was doing what he thought was best for the firm, for her.

And no doubt Dan Harland would be the best man for the firm. She had to respect his brains, his expertise, his authority. Married to her, he would have a strong stake in the firm and he would do his best for it. If she refused to marry him she was in a sense challenging him to take the firm from her, and although she could not see any way in which he could harm the firm there might be a way, and she did not rule out the possibility that he would find that way. There was a dark, ruthless streak in him, as she had seen at their first meeting.

He was using her, but why shouldn't she in turn use him? Marcus was no fool. Dan Harland was the perfect man for the job. She could trust him to govern the firm for her. They would each be getting something out of this marriage.

If only, she thought with a suddenly tense excitement, if only it did not involve marriage ...

She had stopped running and he had caught up with her, but the dark shadow was not lifted. She was petrified. He could engulf her, crush her. She knew it. If she once gave in to him she would never be free again. He could set light to her and consume her. The violence of her own feelings already made her shake. If the mere contemplation of his lovemaking could do that to her when he was not even in the same room, what would it do to her to lie in his arms? He was a rapacious cormorant of a man. For years she had been terrified of emotional commitment, aware that the depths of her own response could be shattering, but none of the men whom she had evaded in the past had had Dan Harland's ability to send her crazy. She had suspected it from the start, but in Greece she had come face to face with the reality of it, going up like straw in his arms, as though he had only to touch her with one finger to make her burn. It had always pleased and relieved her that in other men's arms she could feel coolly in control of herself. She could not have said that after those moments above the brilliant blue sea on the road to Epidaurus.

From the beginning she had feared him. From those moments in Greece she had felt panic lurking at the back of her mind.

Any other man, she thought, and she could hope to manage this mock marriage calmly enough. But him ... she was helpless against him.

'Oh, Marcus,' she groaned aloud to herself. 'What are you doing to me?'

# CHAPTER SIX

LAURA had not looked forward to telling her father about the proposed marriage, but when she went in to his flower-banked little room he listened, bright-eyed and eager, as she nervously told him her news.

'Clever girl,' he added approvingly. 'Why didn't that occur to me? Trust a woman to use her head in a tight spot!'

She stared, open-mouthed. 'Then ... you don't mind?'

'Mind? Of course not. It solves everything. I was worried about leaving you to cope with the swine, but you've pulled our chestnuts out of the fire beautifully.' He flushed, smiling. 'Just make sure Marcus ties the shares up as tight as a drum. The best idea is to have them put in trust for your children. Even Dan Harland wouldn't try to cheat his own children.'

Her colour rose like wildfire in her cheeks. She swallowed. But her father did not notice her reaction. He was too busy laughing, rubbing his hands together. 'We've got him now,' he said in satisfaction. 'He's our man at last. Why didn't I think of it before? As your husband he's tied to our coat tails for good.'

She looked at him wryly. 'Marcus is delighted,' she said.

Bitterness entered Jimmy's voice. 'I bet he is,' he

said. 'My dear father thinks the sun shines out of Dan Harland.' He looked at her with pleading. 'Cut Harland down to size for me, baby. You've got him now. I want to see him pay for every snub he's given me.'

Laura stood up and kissed him lightly. 'Just get better, darling. Don't think about anything else.' Jimmy's vindictive hatred for Dan made her feel slightly sick. Her own reactions to the man came nowhere near her father's brooding jealousy. Jimmy dimly realised that Dan was worth a dozen of him and he both feared and envied him. The malice in his face disturbed and dismayed her.

She had returned to work that day to find the building buzzing with the news of her engagement. Smiling, knowing faces turned to watch her as she moved around the offices. Some of the more senior employees had stopped her to congratulate her and admire her ring, blinking at the size of it. Dan had not stinted when he bought it. It flashed on her hand like blue fire, catching her own eyes whenever her hand moved.

When Olivia Hamilton came into her office with a pile of letters she gave Laura a cool, guarded smile beneath which Laura saw quite clearly the shadow of jealousy. 'Congratulations,' she said, eyeing the ring. 'Of course we were all expecting it, it's no surprise. I've always known Dan would go to the top.'

Laura smiled with barbed irritation, reading the hidden meaning, the cold insinuation. Dan had clearly never hidden from Olivia that he planned to marry her, nor disguised his reasons, and that made her coldly angry.

'Oh, I'm sure he will run my firm very efficiently

for me,' she said sweetly, and saw a faint frown pleat Olivia's temples. The great blue eyes surveyed her and she could tell that Olivia was wondering whether her own darts had hit a target or whether Laura was immune.

Dan took her to lunch. In the taxi she said casually, 'Now that you're getting your own way I presume I can hope to resume my private life without further interference?'

The dark head turned and the grey eyes contemplated her unsmilingly. 'Which means what?'

'That you have blocked some of my relationships in the past, and I see no reason why you should go on doing so.'

'Are you talking about Laxey?' he asked coolly. 'Because if you are, I thought it was understood that you wouldn't be seeing him again.'

'I know you demanded it,' she said bitingly. 'But Joe's an old friend and I refuse to give up my friendships on your command.'

His mouth indented. 'Marcus will expect it.'

'I've already made myself a human sacrifice for Marcus's sake,' she retorted. 'How much more am I supposed to do for him?'

The stony face tightened as she spoke and his eyes iced over. 'Do you imagine you could go on seeing Laxey without causing gossip? People would talk themselves hoarse.'

'Do you really expect me to turn myself into a nun just because I've gone through a charade of marriage with you?'

He gave her a mirthless smile. 'Keep away from Laxey or you'll regret it,' he said, and now the threat was open in his voice.

'You can't do a thing,' she said softly, smiling. 'Neither to me nor to Joe.'

He leaned back, arms folded, casual and blank-faced, but she felt her spine tingle as she met those frozen grey eyes. 'I'll break him,' he said as softly as she had spoken. 'I'll use any weapon I can find and when I've finished with him he'll wish I'd cut his throat.'

She shivered, half believing the threat, but laughed defiantly. 'Very impressive, but Joe's a wealthy man.'

'I know all about Laxey,' he said, breaking into her words. 'I've made a very careful study of him. He would be disconcerted if he knew just how much of his business affairs are known to me ... some of them would be of great interest to the tax authorities.'

Laura looked at him sharply and he met her eyes without a flicker of expression. She frowned. Once or twice Joe had hinted to her that he was involved in some very clever, if doubtful, business, but he had never expanded on the subject and she had never enquired too closely, seeing that he preferred to leave it all shrouded in mystery.

When she was silent Dan's mouth twisted wryly. 'I see you're convinced.'

'Joe is an honest man,' she said firmly, sure that she was right in that.

Dan shrugged. 'I don't say he isn't ... just that he hasn't always been very scrupulous about his business methods and if any of his dealings came to light he could be ... shall we say ... embarrassed?'

'That's blackmail,' she said bitterly.

'Yes,' he said, and smiled in that cold way of his.

'I don't claim to be any more scrupulous myself, but I think I'm more careful than Laxey. He should have buried his corpses rather more deeply.'

'You leave nothing to chance,' she said slowly.

'Only a fool does,' he shrugged.

'You'll have the firm,' she said in a low, furious voice. 'Why can't you leave me alone now?'

He watched her, his face expressionless. 'I've been sitting in on Marcus's meetings with his lawyer. Have you seen his will?'

She shook her head.

Dan smiled briefly. 'Marcus is a shrewd old man. He's tied up the firm very neatly in trust for our children.' His eyes met hers and held them, watching as the colour ran up her face. 'And they'll be my children, Laura, not Joe Laxey's.'

She swallowed, shuddering. 'My God, you ...' Her voice broke off as the words jammed up in her mind.

'I don't trust you, my dear Laura,' he said softly. 'You're a little bitch under that sweet smile. It might amuse you to palm off another man's children on me, but it sure as hell would not amuse me ... so take warning. I will not put up with seeing any other man within a mile of you.' He pushed his hands into his pockets, lying back, a sudden taunt in his smile. 'Until, that is, you've given me a safe number of heirs ... shall we say three? I think three would be a safe number. After that,' he shrugged, 'you can please yourself.'

Laura was white and inwardly raging, her breath coming hard. 'I'd like to kill you,' she muttered huskily. 'I've never wanted to kill anyone before—

but then I've never hated anyone the way I hate you!'

Dan laughed under his breath. 'At least you're not indifferent,' he said mockingly. 'It will make our nights interesting. There's nothing I enjoy as much as a fight.'

Her face flooded with colour and her eyes flashed almost purple, their shade much darker with the temper which was engulfing her. Dan stared at her with those narrowed, glittering eyes, then leaned forward and kissed her briefly, very hard, his mouth bruising, just as the taxi stopped. She had no time to say anything. He moved away from her and she dived out into the street, in such a state that she almost ran away from him, but as if he could read her every thought he was beside her, a hand holding her arm, while he paid the taxi driver and then guided her into the restaurant.

The weeks to their wedding passed heavily for her. Marcus was making a triumphant show of it. He would hear no suggestion of a quiet wedding. He meant the world to see how brilliantly his granddaughter was marrying. She could not have chosen any man who would have delighted him as Dan Harland did. Alone with her one day, Marcus said happily, 'He reminds me of myself when I was young. Dan's going a long way, Laura. The firm will grow under him.'

Even if he has to cut throats to do it, she thought grimly. She was weary of all the fuss. She had spent hours having fittings for her dress. She had bought a trousseau at Marcus's insistence. She had unwrapped wedding presents and gazed in dismay at a line of toasters, silver cruets and trays, tea sets, linen and other household items. Had she been an ordinary bride, no doubt, she would have revelled in it all, but she hated every minute of it.

A week before the wedding Dan told her he had found a house for them in Kent, a modernised Georgian cottage in a small but pretty garden.

'But I thought you were looking for a flat in town,' she said with dismay. It had seemed far the most appropriate home for them and the idea of living in a country home with him sent shivers down her back. It made of their marriage something more permanent, somehow, and she was against the idea.

He said calmly, 'I saw this place advertised and liked the look of it. We'll drive out and see it this afternoon.'

She went with him in a prickly mood, determined to dislike it, but found herself irritatingly charmed by the uneven rambling building, the whitewashed walls charmingly individual, the crazy paving paths around it somehow delightful. An old mill wheel had been set among the broken stones and the cottage was called Mill Wheel Cottage. 'It was built for a miller,' Dan explained, 'in the middle of the eighteenth century. It had fallen into ruin, but the previous owner did it up himself.'

She stood in the spacious main bedroom staring out at the green Kentish countryside, her face sombre. Dan leaned on the windowsill, watching her. 'What do you think?' he asked.

'It's lovely,' she said, and wished she could have said she hated it. She had wanted to refuse to take the house, but honesty compelled her to admit she loved it.

There were two other bedrooms. Dan glanced around one and said lightly, 'This would make a pretty nursery.'

Laura flushed and ignored him, but his teasing eyes followed her as she turned away. On the drive back to London she closed her eyes and he said to her suddenly, 'You look worn out. Is Marcus harrying you?'

'What do you expect me to look like? I'm hardly a joyful bride,' she snapped, and then wished she hadn't because Dan was the first person to notice or care that she was tired and depressed. Her depression was growing as the time passed. She felt grey as she got up in the mornings.

He turned his face towards her, his eyes brittle. 'You might at least try to look less as if you're going to be executed than married,' he said through his teeth.

She gave him a false, over-bright beam. 'Like that, you mean? Of course. I'll smile like a lighthouse if that's what you want.'

Dan's eyes flashed. 'One of these days you're going to push me too far, Laura, and when I'm angry I can get very nasty.'

'You mean you can be nastier than you usually are?'

'Very funny,' he said, and after that he said nothing else until they got back to London.

Renata flew over to be her bridesmaid. She had had her bridesmaid's dress made in Geneva to a pattern Laura had sent. It matched those of the two little girls who were to walk behind Renata. They were Dan's sister's children and Laura had only met them once. She had been whisked off one Sunday to have tea with their mother and father, Dan's only close relatives. His parents were dead, she had learnt, and his sister, Pam, was the only one of his family he ever saw. Pam was a lively, intelligent woman in her thirties with Dan's grey eyes and dark colouring. Her husband, Ralph, was a stockbroker with little conversation, but he and Pam seemed very happy. During the hours she spent there Laura felt it a strain trying to seem happy. Dan's attitude was calmly affectionate and Pam did not seem to notice any lack in the way they behaved to each other.

Being with Renata was worse. When they met at Heathrow, Renata shrieked, 'You double-crosser, you! I thought we were going to be spinsters all our lives!' And while Laura was laughing, added, 'So what did you do to him, the terrible Dan Harland? What spell did you use? I remember what a cold fish he was to me... I can't believe it. You must have slipped him an aphrodisiac!'

Laura laughed again and shrugged, finding it bitterly hard to lie to her best friend but unable to tell the truth. 'He's... special,' she admitted.

'Oh, I remember that,' Renata agreed, tongue in cheek. 'I thought so myself, but I made as much impression on him as a fork would have on a concrete wall!'

When they had lunch with Dan next day he went out of his way to charm her, his smile giving that cold, handsome face an allure which maddened Laura. Renata was dazzled. She stared at him throughout the meal with goggling eyes, and afterwards groaned to Laura, 'I could go for him, you know, really fall ... you lucky beast! He makes Max look like a non-starter.'

The night before the wedding Laura and Renata spent the evening together at Renata's hotel. They ate a leisurely dinner, talked and giggled over the wine, went up to Renata's room and sat about until the small hours gossiping and reliving old affairs. When she said goodnight Laura was in a fighting mood. The wine had gone to her head. In midjourney she suddenly leaned forward and told the taxi driver to take her to Dan's flat instead of her own, and when it dropped her, marched up to his door with a flushed, wild-eyed face.

She leaned on the door bell and after persistent ringing it jerked away from her as Dan pulled the door open. She fell forward and he caught her, his hands under her armpits.

'I am not going to marry you,' she enunciated very clearly, pulling back to glare at him. 'Do you hear? I damned well refuse! I hate the sight of you. Take the company, if you want it that much, but you're not getting me along with it!' She had had the words burning in her head for days and now they shot out at a frantic rate, crisp and clear and unwavering, and when she had said them she felt sleepy, drained. She swayed, turning to go.

Dan's hands caught her arms and yanked her through the door into his flat. She struggled, flailing her hands. 'Take your hands off me, will you? I can't bear having you touch me!'

'How much have you drunk?' he asked, apparently amused.

'Never you mind!' she snapped. Her head was going round. She leaned forward, eyes closing, and found his body supporting her. 'Oh, my head!' she groaned.

He closed the door with one hand and lifted her like a baby, one arm around her back, the other under her legs. Laura could not open her eyes. Her head was swimming dizzily. She was aware faintly that he was carrying her, then that he had lowered her on to something soft and comfortable. 'Oooh!' she moaned, as his hands moved over her, lifting her, removing her coat. She was only aware of his movements as irritations in her desperate need to sleep. Dimly she felt her dress being removed, then she felt him move away, and with the rapidity of the click of a shutter she was asleep.

Some time during the night she began to dream. The dreams were intense. Burningly pleasurable, she was submitting to Dan's lovemaking, groaning under the smooth caress of his hands as they moved over her, stroking her bare skin. It was so deeply real that she moaned aloud as those long fingers felt their way along her shoulders, investigating the hollows between her fine bones, exploring the warm curve of her throat before slowly descending to the rounded flesh of her breasts, fondling them in a languorous tactile sensuality which made her twist, half sobbing, to turn her face into his neck and kiss his skin passionately. The sensation of finding her mouth against his flesh woke her with violent abruptness.

It was no dream. She was lying naked in his arms and he was engrossed in a slow, sensual exploration of her body.

Their eyes met and scarlet swam up her face. 'Oh,

God,' she muttered, pushing him away fiercely. 'You ... you bastard!'

There was red colour along his cheekbones. His eyes were hot between the heavy lids. Silently he pulled her back into his arms and then she began to fight in earnest because her own senses told her he was fiercely aroused. He might have planned to marry her to acquire the company, but his body told her now that he wanted her, that his desire for possession did not end with the control of the firm.

'No!' she gasped, her pulses thudding like steam-hammers in her own ears.

'If you're not going to marry me I can't make you,' he said hoarsely. 'But I sure as hell can make you give me what you've given Laxey and God knows who else.'

'Why, you ...' Outrage and insulted pride thickened her voice. She dug her nails into his bare shoulders, her eyes brilliant with rage. 'Is that what you think?'

He lay still, holding her with those powerful fingers, staring into her eyes. 'Haven't you?'

Her face was flaming. 'No, I haven't,' she said with a quiver in her voice.

'None of them?' he asked tautly.

'None of them,' she said in a voice which almost hissed. 'And I wouldn't give you a spent match, Dan Harland. Anything you get from me you're going to have to take by force, and I'll scream the place down if you so much as try!'

He leant back, a peculiar smile on the hard mouth. 'My God, you provocative little bitch, you certainly had me fooled! Ever since I saw you come out of that fellow's arms in Geneva I've thought ...'

He broke off and she snapped her teeth together.

'I've gathered what you thought, and you were wrong!'

'Not even Laxey?' He was watching her with the heavy lids well down over his eyes.

'I told you ... no!'

'Well, I'm damned,' he muttered.

Laura wriggled backwards and slid off the bed, dragging the sheet with her, draping it around herself. 'Now I'm getting dressed and getting out of here,' she said.

'I'll drive you down as planned,' he told her, and she stood there, staring at him.

'I told you ...'

'Laura, if you think I'm letting you get away, you can think again. You're going to marry me if I have to deliver you tied in a brown paper parcel to that church.'

She stamped her foot like an infuriated child, her colour vivid. 'I don't want to marry you! Can't you get it into your thick head?'

He laughed and there was that charm in his face again, maddening her. 'You know your problem, Laura? You weren't spanked enough as a little girl. I'll have to remedy that.'

She backed as though afraid he would carry out his threat there and then and he laughed again. 'Shall I help you dress?' he asked teasingly.

'You dare!' she snapped.

'I took your clothes off,' he pointed out. 'You seemed grateful for my help then.'

'I was ...' She broke off and added after a pause, 'I wasn't well.'

'You were drunk,' he corrected, grinning.

'That's a lie! It's just that ... wine makes me ill.'

'You lovely little liar,' he said, moving closer, his eyes soft. Laura backed again and he stopped, shrugging.

'All right, get dressed. We'll have some breakfast, then pick up your case and drive down to Marcus's.'

While she was dressing with shaking hands she realised it was almost seven. The dawn light was paling the sky. She had been in Dan's bed for hours and what had happened while she slept? She shuddered, remembering her dreams. They had been blindingly exciting. He had been touching her, caressing her. And they had not been dreams. While she was drowning in heavy sleep he had removed all her clothes and enjoyed her body. She had been conscious at some level of her mind of what he was doing to her. She had to have been, because in those dreams of hers she had been fully responsive, abandoning herself to his stroking hands, and there had been no repulsion, no rejection. When she woke up she had been entwined with him, her mouth against his strong throat.

Oh, God, she groaned. She felt as though he had entered her subconscious, raped her mind.

He drove her to her flat where she collected her packed suitcase, then went on to pick up Renata, as planned, to drive them both down to Marcus's house. Marcus had protested that they should not see each other on their wedding day, but both she and Dan had been determined not to allow outmoded superstition to cloud their minds. Now, seated beside him in the fast car, she wondered miserably if she should have followed Marcus's advice and not seen him.

Glancing at him in secret, sideways inspection, she thought him almost unbearably attractive in his formal morning suit. The closely tailored set of the dark material suited him, that handsome, cold face thrown into relief. As if becoming aware of her gaze he slipped an oblique look at her and she flushed, looking away. He was beyond her comprehension. Then her blood quickened as memory flashed back those moments in his arms. Just for once she had seen him with that mask removed, and although never at any time could she comfort herself by thinking that he had been out of control, he had had to fight for his self-control. He had struggled with desire for her and she had watched him. It was a shred of comfort to take her into their strange, enforced marriage.

Marcus met them all at his front door, shooed Dan away with an irritated shake of his head, and rushed both Laura and Renata upstairs to get ready for the wedding that afternoon. The house was crammed with people. Laura had to smile and wave to various distant relatives, some of them barely known to her. 'I still think you should have been down here yesterday,' Marcus said crossly. 'This is no way to get married, rushing down from London with the bridegroom with only a few hours to spare.'

'Don't fuss,' she smiled, kissing his wrinkled cheek. 'Has Jimmy got here yet?'

'He's resting in his own room,' Marcus told her. 'One of the nurses came with him. Fine-looking woman, strong-minded. Nice of her to give up time off to escort Jimmy like that.'

Laura went along to see her father and found him reading a sporting paper which he guiltily pushed under his pillow with a grin at her.

'Big day, baby,' he said as she kissed him, then looked at her clothes in surprise. 'Shouldn't you be dressing?'

'Yes, and I'm going to, but I wanted to see you first,' she said, then turned as the door opened and a woman came into the room. With a start of surprise Laura recognised the Sister who had nursed Jimmy at his worst. The woman gave her a friendly smile.

'I hope you'll be very happy, my dear,' she said. 'Do you need any help?'

'That's kind, but no, thank you,' said Laura, smiling back. 'It's very kind of you to look after Jimmy like this.'

She caught the quick exchange of glances between them and registered a wry amusement. So, she thought, Jimmy up to his old tricks again! And the woman seemed so sensible, too, a level-headed and intelligent woman. She talked to them both lightly for a while, then left them together, and when she got back to her own room Renata, in a fine apricot silk slip, looked at her sharply and asked with a grin, 'What is funny?'

'Jimmy,' Laura told her. 'Funny how sensible women can fall for that little-boy idiocy of his!'

Renata looked intrigued. 'Really? Tell ... who?'

'Never mind,' said Laura, laughing. 'Well, I suppose I must start getting ready.'

Renata frowned at her. 'You sound almost reluctant ... Laura, is something up?'

'No, no,' Laura said quickly, giving her a bright smile. 'Just ... bridal nerves.'

'Oh, those,' said Renata with a wink, whisked off

and came back with an opened bottle of champagne and two glasses. Laura stared, eyes wide.

'Where did that come from?'

'Your grandfather,' said Renata. 'Wise old man!'

Cunning old man, Laura thought, accepting a glass. The dry sparkle of the wine hit the back of her nose and she sneezed, making Renata laugh.

'That's lucky,' she said.

'Lucky? Why?'

'Old custom of my country,' Renata said cheerfully, sipping as she wandered around in her slip. 'But then with a man like Dan Harland for your groom you don't need luck, darling.'

That, thought Laura, is just what I do need, if you did but realise it. Luck in gallons. And her nerves leapt like wildfire as she contemplated becoming Dan Harland's wife. She had never expected to marry anyone. Her love life had been quite complicated enough—for most of the time since she became an adult she had been fending men off with all the charm she could manage so that even after she had refused them firmly she had always managed to keep them as friends. Her fear of the suffocating possession which love implied to her had stifled any emotional responses she had ever felt stirring towards anyone. While she slowly dressed for her wedding she frowned over her own emotions. She realised the oddness of her reactions, but knowing oneself was only half the problem. One had to be able to act to alter the way one felt, and that Laura could not do.

Renata stood back to stare at her and smiled radiantly. 'Darling, I could cry!'

'No, don't,' Laura urged, laughing too sharply.

'You might start me off!'

'You look beautiful! Oh, I'm green with envy!'

Laura glanced almost reluctantly at her own reflection in the long mirror. The tight-fitting white lace gown clung to her body, the smooth heavy satin sheath of the undergown fitting from her breasts to her feet, her flesh showing faintly pink through the lace over shoulders and arms. Her hair curled round her face, framing it, and the flowing lace of the veil gave her a medieval simplicity, held in place by a crown of pearls and tiny waxen white flowers.

Marcus had insisted on a traditional wedding and only now did Laura consider the symbolic trappings of it all, shivering at the thought that after this ceremony she would belong to Dan Harland.

She wanted to cry out in protest, to refuse to go through with it, but she knew she did not have the necessary courage to stop it now. With the inexorability of a tank the time was rolling forward and soon she would stand at the altar beside the man she hated, making the ritual responses, giving herself into his keeping.

'You're white,' Renata said anxiously, watching her. 'I know what you need ... some more champagne!'

Laura took the offered glass and drained it thirstily while Renata stared at her almost in dismay.

'Are you that scared?' she asked. 'Darling, I never expected you to be so wound up! You're always so calm and sure of yourself!'

How could she be calm, Laura thought, when Dan Harland was waiting for her like a wolf at the door?

Then Marcus came in and looked at her with tears in his eyes. Renata tactfully slid out of the room and Laura went into her grandfather's arms, sobbing on his shoulder, while he heavily patted her as if she were a hurt child. 'There, there ... I remember your grandmother crying on our wedding day,' he said, smiling. 'Women always cry at weddings—I don't know why. Your grandmother cried at your father's wedding ... all the women did. I heard them sniffing and gulping all over the church.'

Laura giggled helplessly. 'Oh, I hope they don't at mine!'

'They will,' he said. 'They always do.'

She looked up at him. 'Are you sure Jimmy's well enough to give me away? We don't want to try his strength.'

'He wants to do it,' Marcus said firmly. 'And it's his right.'

He fumbled in an inside pocket and produced a flat box. 'I want you to wear this, darling. It was your grandmother's ... you've made me very happy with this marriage. Dan is the man I wanted for you, and it's given me a new lease of life to see you two together.' He moved behind her and tremblingly slid a pearl necklace round her throat, the pearls smooth and pinkish, their light glowing against her warm skin. She put a finger on them and smiled at him.

'Oh, Marcus, they're lovely! Thank you!'

He kissed her again. 'No, thank you, Laura. I can rest easy knowing Dan will always look after you and the firm.'

She looked at him with loving wryness. 'I'm glad you're happy.'

Then Jimmy came in on his nurse's arm, moving very slowly, his body stooped. He grinned at Laura and made a face of amazement.

'Can this be my little girl? What a picture!' He smiled as she kissed him, but the emotional moment she had shared with Marcus made Jimmy's light teasing almost meaningless. All her life Jimmy had evaded responsibility, eluded her affection, and now she realised that her grandfather had been her true father all her life. She was older than Jimmy in her mind and heart. He was still a child, playing at life. He had neither the inclination nor the capacity for real love. She had always blamed his shallow nature on her mother's early death, but now she guessed that Jimmy had not even deeply cared for his wife, for anyone. She looked at him, loved him and despaired of him, and, looking at Marcus, she caught the shadow of her own sadness over him in that old face. No wonder Marcus had turned so urgently to Dan for the strength and depth he had never got from his own son. Poor Marcus, she thought.

The drive to the little church went too quickly for her. She sat beside Jimmy, her veil over her white face, trembling. 'Nice to be out in the air,' commented Jimmy, staring out at the countryside, grinning. He had no suspicion of her feelings, she realised, and was glad. Marcus might have been more percipient and she did not want anyone to know how terrified she was just now.

On Jimmy's arm she walked down the aisle, biting her lip, glad of the protcetion of her drawn veil, a smothered sob shaking her body.

Dan looked round, but she evaded his eyes, her own downcast. The service proceeded and she heard her own voice huskily whispering the responses, marvelling that she could speak when her throat seemed closed with fear.

Dan put back her veil deftly and she felt his grey eyes swiftly rake her pale face. Then he kissed her and she shuddered at the cold touch of his mouth. He glanced at her again before moving away and she knew he was angry. He had noted her instinctive recoil from him and he did not like it.

## CHAPTER SEVEN

LAURA found the wedding reception an ordeal. She stood with Dan at the door of the large hall, her veil thrown back, a polite smile pinned to her face, welcoming the guests as they arrived, while all the time her whole body was taut with consciousness of Dan at her side, aware of every breath he took, every movement he made. From time to time she looked at the gold ring he had placed on her finger and she shivered. Symbol of possession, she thought, wishing she had the courage to pull it off and throw it down at his feet. Instead she stood there, making the usual small talk, thanking people for gifts, accepting congratulations and good wishes. And when Dan turned to her and drew her into what he was saying to someone she would smile and smile, knowing that he saw beneath her smile to the shrinking within her, and that he was coldly, silently furious with her.

Pam and her husband kissed her, talking brightly, and brought along Dan's great-aunt Joan, a very small person in an old-fashioned black hat with coiled wires which fluttered on it when she moved her head, making her look like a bee, especially since she wore a yellow dress and had a buzzing, cheerful little voice. Laura liked her at sight, drawn by her very sharp, kind brown eyes and the dimples which were still retained in her withered cheeks. 'You must come and stay with me,' said Aunt Joan. 'Dan used to stay when he was little. Do you remember, Dan?'

'Vividly,' he said, and smiled at her, surprising Laura by the warmth and charm of his smile. 'You had a cat as big as a great Dane who could ring the door bell when he wanted to come in.'

Aunt Joan's eyes twinkled. 'His great-great-grandson has inherited the trick!'

Laura laughed. 'You're joking!'

'No, no, my dear ... Samson died twenty years ago, but he left quite a few descendants and I've two of them now, Solly and Mab. My next door neighbour, Mrs Hunt, is keeping an eye on them for me. I never leave my cats for long. Fastidious creatures, cats. They like their home comforts and they don't like strangers.'

'Did they like Dan?' Laura asked a little teasingly, and the grey eyes switched to her face, a curious expression in them.

Aunt Joan's mouth twitched. 'Samson detested him,' she said. 'Dan tied a bell on his neck and it drove poor Samson wild. He arched his back and spat whenever he set eyes on Dan after that.'

Laura's blue eyes were innocent as her glance shifted to Dan. 'How unusual,' she said sweetly.

'Unusual?' Aunt Joan asked, perplexed.

'For cats to dislike him,' Laura explained. 'They usually seem to follow him around.' Her eyes flicked briefly to Olivia Hamilton and then back to Dan. 'Quite devotedly.'

His eyes narrowed and a smile touched his mouth. While Aunt Joan moved on he whispered, 'You little shrew!'

And Laura pretended not to hear.

Olivia's presence had irritated Laura, who had not thought of inviting her. Clearly Dan, however, had done so, although very few of their employees had been invited.

When Joe arrived, immaculate in a dark lounge suit, his brown hair smoothly brushed down, Laura thanked him for his wedding present in a nervous tone, aware of Dan's attentive presence at her side. The arrival of Joe's present had begun a cold argument between them only a few days earlier. Dan had watched her unpack it and taken one of the handsome set of seventeenth-century Italian plates, his face cold. 'Generous of him,' he had commented through tight lips. His eyes rose to Laura's face, piercing her flushed features. 'Collectors' items! We are not accepting them. Joe Laxey is not a member of your family. I do not take gifts this expensive from a mere friend.'

She had said angrily, 'They're meant for me, not you,' and Dan had retorted icily, 'I'm aware of that, thank you. Send them back.'

'No!' she had said sharply, and the quarrel might have flared into open warfare if Marcus had not walked in, picked up one of the plates and exclaimed rapturously over them. Dan had left without a word.

Now she saw Joe move on with relief, having been afraid Dan might speak to him about the plates, and Dan gave her one long, frozen look before turning to the next guest.

Later she and Dan opened the dancing after the leisurely wedding breakfast, a formal smile pinned on both their faces. They only meant to stay another hour and she was both eager and reluctant to get away, feeling the strain of the occasion yet dreading the moment when she would be alone with Dan at last. He murmured a few polite remarks and she as politely answered them, but by the spark in the grey eyes she knew he was not deceived by her outward calm.

When their dance ended she was glad to find herself surrounded by members of her own family, all talking in nostalgic terms of other family occasions. Jimmy was sipping some wine, his nurse eyeing him chidingly. Laura caught her reproving eye and smiled at her. Dan moved away and a while later she saw him dancing with Olivia. A peculiar fierce pain stabbed through her and she looked hurriedly away.

Joe moved through the crowd and smiled down at her, holding out his hand, and she moved off with him among the dancers.

'You held out on me,' he said quietly. 'I thought you were against the marriage tie.'

'This is different,' she said lightly, and smiled.

'That's what they all say,' Joe commented, his eyes on her face. 'I really thought you meant it, Laura. I had you down as the sort who likes to be free.'

Her colour mounted as she looked away and Joe kissed her cheek softly, murmuring, 'O.K., I shan't say another word. I believe you were the one girl I ever met who talked my language, but I'm a good loser. Harland's quite a guy and I envy him.'

Laura smiled, half tearful, touched by the words, and as she looked over his shoulder found herself looking into Dan's watchful, cold eyes. Her colour deepened to a hot scarlet and she quickly looked away.

Just before they left she danced with Dan again. She had avoided the necessity by dancing with a succession of her relatives, but he trapped her while she was talking to Marcus and dared not refuse. Under her grandfather's delighted, happy eyes she went into Dan's arms and whirled away, her full white skirts flying.

While they danced his grey eyes lowered to her shoulders, observed the brief glimpse of white skin left bare by her wedding gown, dropped to skim over her breasts, observing the quick rise and fall of her body beneath the tautly stretched material. She felt heat rise in her throat. His eyes came back to her face and she looked at him with hatred.

He had booked a villa in Tuscany for two weeks, and the thought of that time ahead made her tense and furious. He was looking at her as if he were undressing her and she was both angry and excited.

Dan had not said a word. She could find nothing to say, either. She was trembling and he knew it. His fingers stroked down over her back and then suddenly flattened, pressing her body against his.

'Don't,' she whispered huskily, pulling away.

He made no attempt to repeat the movement. A moment later the dance ended and she was freed. Her legs were weak as she walked away.

On the flight to Italy she faced the fact that she was locked with him in an intimacy she had not anticipated. It was not that she would see him all the time. It was that she was constantly on the verge of complete surrender and Dan knew it. His eyes told her he knew. He never said a word, but she knew his tactics now. She was deeply aware of the slow, silent, remorseless pursuit. Once it had merely been his desire to marry her and by that marriage capture the control of the company. Now it was herself he wanted to possess; she had known it ever since the night before the wedding. She had aroused Dan. His eyes glittered with desire as he looked at her and he would not give up until he was satisfied.

The villa lay in the green hills above Florence. White, low, rambling, it was surrounded with green cypress and a terraced olive grove lay beyond.

Laura was terrified that on their wedding night Dan would come to her and demand her surrender, but after they had eaten he sat listening to music, nodding when she got up and went to bed alone. She lay awake for a long time, but he did not come, and she fell asleep, torn between relief and disappointment.

They drove around Florence's spreading, enveloping countryside and she fell in love with it. It had a beautifully familiar aspect, reminding her of all the Renaissance pictures she had ever seen, that shadowy green background to all the religious paintings of the time, so that Christ's birth seemed most naturally to have happened in a farmyard in Tuscany with the blue-hazed hills and dark green cypresses fading into the distance.

They walked around the city for hours, visiting the museums and galleries, eating slices of cool watermelon from street vendors, sitting at street cafés watching the floods of tourists drift by like autumn leaves.

Sometimes as they walked Dan would rest his hand on her waist, a light, cool touch which brought fever to her veins.

When they ate in the villa they chose salad for convenience. Dan helped her prepare it and they moved around the marble-floored kitchen in comparative harmony, working together. One very hot day they decided to stay in the garden. Laura put on a bikini and lay on a lounger with dark glasses shielding her eyes, sunbathing. Dan had a few phone calls to make, but when he came out later he was in black swimming trunks, his muscled body gleaming under the burning sun.

He halted beside the lounger, his eyes slowly wandering over the seductive curves of her body, and she felt herself blushing heatedly.

'Like a drink?' he asked, and she quickly nodded.

He walked back into the villa while she stared after him, angrily aware of being aroused by the lithe bronzed body, prickling with sexual attraction despite her dislike and fear of him.

He returned with a tall glass of lime spiked with gin for her and lay down beside her in a matching lounger, holding a glass of whisky and soda which he sipped, looking at her over the rim.

'I've just been speaking to Marcus,' he said.

She half sat. 'Something wrong? Jimmy?'

His mouth turned down. 'No, there's nothing wrong with Jimmy.' He stared at her unreadably. 'You care quite a bit for that precious father of yours, don't you?'

'He's my father,' she said flatly. 'What did Marcus want?'

'There's been some sort of move on the market ... he suspects someone of buying up our shares. There could be a take-over bid on the way.'

She frowned. 'How could there? Marcus owns fifty-one per cent.'

Dan stared stolidly at her. 'Not quite,' he said. 'Not now.'

She was puzzled. 'He does! He ...'

'He handed over ten per cent of his shares to Jimmy the day you married me,' Dan told her, watching her intently.

Laura's eyes opened wide. She sat up fully, her drink almost slipping from her grasp. 'He did what?'

'It was Jimmy's price to agree to your marriage settlement,' Dan told her. 'Why do you think he so calmly accepted the suggestion that Marcus should leave control of the firm to us?'

'But it means you won't have control, after all,' Laura protested. 'And Jimmy might ...' She broke off, biting her lip.

'Go on,' Dan said curtly.

Their eyes met. She was white. 'Jimmy is capable of selling those shares if the price is right,' she whispered.

Dan nodded. 'Yes. Your precious father is more

than capable of it. Marcus has tried to get in touch with him today and surprise, surprise... Jimmy has vanished. Odd coincidence, isn't it?'

She put down her glass, shivering. 'Oh, why was Marcus such a fool? He knows...'

'He knows he can't trust Jimmy further than he can see him,' Dan agreed coldly.

'Then why...'

'Marcus desperately wanted our marriage,' Dan explained. 'He couldn't make himself believe that Jimmy would do anything like this to you.' His mouth twisted sardonically. 'Oh, Marcus knew Jimmy would like to stick a knife in me.' His eyes flashed ice-grey at her. 'A characteristic he shares with you, my darling wife. But Marcus thought he could trust Jimmy where you were concerned.'

Laura tried to think, her eyes darkened. 'We must go back,' she said.

'No!' Dan said sharply. 'We're on our honeymoon and we stay here.'

'But you can't leave Marcus to fight this alone. He's a sick old man.'

'Marcus can deal with it,' Dan assured her.

'You can't be serious!'

'Perfectly,' he said.

'Marcus is only just recovering from another heart attack! He's in no condition to cope with this sort of situation on his own!'

'Marcus will cope,' he said without inflection, his face as hard as rock.

She leapt to her feet. 'Well, I'm not staying here while my grandfather and my father fight over the company. I'm going back, whether you come or not!'

She turned and ran back into the villa, her face flushed with anger and disbelief. In her bedroom she pulled down her cases and began to pack, moving from wardrobe to bed quickly, still wearing her bikini, her mind frantic with worry and rage.

The door opened and Dan walked in slowly. Laura ignored him, her back turned to him, pulling down clothes from the racks with shaking hands. A crash made her turn in shock. Dan had swept her cases from the bed and her clothes lay spilled in disarray across the floor.

'What do you think you're doing?' she asked furiously.

He took two steps, his face taut, staring at her slender, golden body with eyes which were no longer unreadable, flame lighting their dark centres.

'No!' she whispered, her throat closing.

He did not bother to answer. The strong, long-fingered hands fastened on her bare arms, yanking her forward, her wild cry of protest ignored. Before she could pull away his mouth relentlessly covered hers with a violence which silenced all resistance, forcing her lips to open beneath his own, raping her mouth, one hand moving up to hold her neck in a vice-like grip, tilting her head so that she could not escape from the hot invasion he was inflicting. She moaned and fought, her hands pressed against his bare chest, but without lifting his mouth from hers he slowly forced her backwards until she overbalanced and fell across the bed. To her dazed senses he seemed like a falling tower as his hard body followed her, crushing her down against the quilt.

Gasping, she struggled, as much against the burning desire he had awoken in herself as against him, kicking and plunging beneath him, her fingers curled like claws. Suddenly her mouth was free. Dan turned his head to look along their locked bodies, watching the movements of her imprisoned figure, and a slow tremor ran through her at the smile which suddenly touched his mouth. He glanced back at her and she could read the expression in his grey eyes. He was enjoying her struggle for freedom. Far from dissuading him, every movement she made was exciting him, making him more urgent.

She stopped fighting, and they stared at each other. Laura felt the slow rough pleasure of his thigh as it forced itself between her own. 'Please,' she whispered shakily, abandoning every attempt to escape except a humiliating plea for mercy. 'Please, Dan, you're frightening me!'

'I'm not going back to England until you're my wife in every sense of the word,' he said thickly.

Her eyes widened. 'Marcus needs you ... the firm ...'

'Damn the firm,' he snapped, his features harsh. The grey eyes flicked over her hungrily. 'I've played a waiting game for months, but I'm not waiting another day, Laura. I want you, and you're going to let me make love to you before you leave this room again.'

The fierce determination in his voice left her helpless. She weakly closed her eyes. He lay watching her without moving for a few moments, then his hands moved, slowly touching her, running down over her body smoothly, stroking and caressing. She abandoned thought of everything but the sweetness of the sensations his hands were arousing in her. She had never known that it could be so exciting to be touched. In the past when men tried to pet her she had irritably pulled away, or submitted without real enjoyment, half amused by their strange desire to kiss or caress her. Now a tactile sensuality was dominating her physically and emotionally.

She was reliving the dreams she had had the night before their wedding, but now she was wildly, burningly awake, and as Dan's hands moved freely over her she felt her skin tingle with pleasure. For months she had been running from him. Now she could not move an inch. With closed eyes and a beating heart she embraced her own destruction, offering herself to his possessing hands.

His fingers deftly unhooked her bikini and removed it. He bent his head and his lips warmly touched her throat, finding the fast-beating pulse at the base of it. Neither of them said a word. The only sounds were the faint sighing groans she had begun to make as her pleasure grew greater.

The violence had died out of him. Now there was no haste in his lovemaking. Sensuous, languid, he was taking his time quite deliberately, and every move he made increased her sexual excitement.

The slow, warm exploration spread to her shoulders, his mouth given free rein. Laura's hand moved abruptly, lying against his dark hair as his head moved down her body, feeling an electric shock at the feel of his thick, warm vital hair under her fingers. She felt his cheek brush one of her breasts, then his mouth gently slid over the white skin until it touched her nipple. She gave a high moan, reacting with panic. 'No, Dan!'

He laughed softly, repeating the caress, his mouth

seductive, lazy. She felt his hands moving down her body, his palms warm against her curved hips. 'Don't be frightened,' he whispered. 'The last thing I want to do is hurt you. Relax, Laura. Don't fight me now.'

Her lids fluttered back and her blue eyes looked wildly at him. 'Dan, I ...'

He slid up her body and his mouth silenced her. The deep-buried heat in her own body seemed to flare out of all control, and she kissed him back hungrily, her hands moving round his back, digging into the smooth muscled body.

She remembered the moment above the sea in Greece when she had turned, blind from the sun, to look at him and seen his face loom through her own dazzled sight, felt the powerful tug of her own desire for him. She had admitted then what her subconscious had known since the day they met. She wanted him. He had set her blazing with hunger from the start.

He began to stroke her again, whispering words softly, their meaning muffled for her as he kissed her soft, rounded breasts, burying his face in them. Seduction, she thought dimly ... he was seducing her, and she had no weapons to fight against him now. Others had tried in the past and she had never felt the slightest desire to succumb to their blandishments, but this man could take whatever he liked and she would not be able to raise a finger to stop him.

He knew it too, she recognised. He was invading every inch of her now, exploring her body boldly, making her give herself up to him, his breathing harsh. Against her, he was trembling, and she felt a shock of eager excitement as she knew that he was as aroused as herself.

At the back of her mind a voice was asking her if she was crazy to let him do this, because he was not saying he loved her, he was not even pretending it. The increasing urgency of his lovemaking was inspired by pure and simple desire, a physical need which was driving him more and more as she submitted to his caresses.

She had given in to his desire to own her family firm and now he was going to take her, too, and the act of ownership which he meant to enforce on her was the one from which she had shrunk all her adult life. That would not have mattered so much since she admitted grimly that she wanted him, too, that he was not going to take a thing she did not want to give him, but in that very fact lay the seed of her fear and panic. It was her own blind submission she feared. She was afraid of her own desperate need for love. Inch by inch over the months, Dan had been gaining on her in her headlong flight from him. Inch by inch she had been ceding him territory in her own mind. The original blanket hatred she had felt had been eaten up over the months as she admitted his charm, his attraction and now his sexual allure for her. Once he had become her lover she was terrified that she would go up like straw, blazing crazily for him, obsessed with him. In early childhood she had learnt to live without love, rejected so far back in life by Jimmy that she had buried the original memory out of sight, but the lessons she had learnt then had stayed with her, hardening like concrete in her brain.

It was dangerous to care for anyone. It was tempting providence. Once one loved, one was vulnerable, one was asking for rejection, humiliation, pain.

She wrenched herself away, moaning, 'No, Dan!' Her high-pitched cry startled him out of his own intent absorption.

He lifted away from her, staring, flushed and breathing hard. She tried to roll away, trembling, but he dragged her back, suddenly angry.

'The hell you do,' he muttered fiercely.

'I can't,' she almost shouted, glaring at him. 'I won't!'

'You can and you will,' muttered Dan between tight teeth, his face hard and angular. 'You've gone too far, you frigid little bitch, and I'm not stopping now.'

Her face was white, her eyes almost demented as his mouth came down to her pulsing throat, hotly kissing the soft skin, then she arched in rejection as his thigh parted hers and his hands slid under her. 'No!' she cried, and the sound sharpened in pain suddenly as the powerful body overwhelmed her. She closed her eyes, groaning, struggling. His breathing came fast and thickly to her. He was kissing her throat, his heart thudding above her as his movements intensified, the strong, driving force taking her beyond her feelings of panic and fear into a new dimension she had not suspected. At first she felt a faint sensation of pleasure and instinctively relaxed, freed from the pain he had at first inflicted. Aware of her softening, he began to kiss her mouth deeply. Laura's hands slid up his chest to his throat, pulling his head down, winding up into his thick hair, her fingers curled in explosive excitement as she began to respond.

He drew away and bent to kiss her breast and she buried her face in his throat, kissing it hotly, moaning incoherently, a piercing tension in her body, aching along her taut bones, a frenzy singing in her blood. It grew with such rapidity that her head fell back on the pillow, her lips parted on a groan of pleasure amounting to anguish. Through her flickering lashes she saw Dan's hard-boned face, flushed and rigid with desire as he looked down at her, the grey eyes flaming so that she wondered how she had ever thought them cold. Now they were molten, burning, and she heard the sound of his smothered groans as if they came from a long way away. Then the pleasure rose to intolerable heights and she lost all consciousness of everything but her own sensations. Once as a child she had had dreams in which she fell from a great height, floating downwards weightlessly, a silent scream on her lips, her stomach clenching in a fierce panic. Now she found the same sensation enclosing her. She was dropping sharply, as if she were in a lift whose cable had snapped, and she was crying out wildly, hanging on to Dan's shoulders, driving her fingernails into his flesh, unaware of any pain she might cause him.

She fell into a silence, a warm, lazy, languid ease which was like the peace of a summer's day. Dan's head dropped on her body, his breathing slowing, his heart settling to a quieter pace. His hands stroked her body gently. She lay, eyes closed, her arms around his neck, feeling the tension, the panic, drain out of her toes.

Dan suddenly turned his face against her cheek. 'Thank you,' he said huskily, his lips moving against her skin.

Something hurt inside her. She didn't answer. Why had he said that? He had spoken as though she had given him some pleasant but unmemorable gift, but it had been the gift of herself and his words stung bitterly, humiliated.

She could not move or she would cry. She would allow him to see how badly he had hurt her, but she must not let him know that. He must never know that while he was taking her body she was giving him her heart, the one gift she had always determined never to bestow on any man. She had not meant to give it. She had fought to withhold it from him, but in the end it had flown from her grasp as though it had wings and now Dan had it in his possession, as he had had her just now, and like the princess in the fairy story she was under the curse which had threatened her all her life. Dan had destroyed her, as she had known he would. She loved him.

When she felt she had the necessary courage she moved, pushing at him. 'Can I get dressed now?' she asked him coldly. 'I presume that now you will let me go to my grandfather?'

He swung the black head to stare at her and the flush on his face hardened while the grey eyes grew freezingly cold. After a moment, he said flatly, 'Why not?'

She moved off the bed and picked up a wrap lying on a chair, tying it with shaking hands. 'Am I going alone or are you coming?'

He gave her a derisive look, meant to underline the amusement with which he viewed her attempts to hide herself from him after all that had happened between them. 'I shall come,' he said coolly, getting up.

Laura looked away from the strong brown muscled body, her throat dry.

'I'll go and pack,' said Dan, sauntering unconcernedly to the door. When it had closed behind him she sank down on the bed and put her head in her hands, weeping like a lost child.

## CHAPTER EIGHT

On the flight back to England she sat beside him on the window side of the plane, staring out at the white undercurrents of the sky, a blue streak floating incandescently in the distance, the diffused brilliance of the sun behind it. Dan shifted in his seat, his newspaper crackling, and she glanced sideways at him, meeting his eyes. He gave her a sudden grin. 'Stop looking so frantic,' he whispered, leaning over.

'Do I?' Her colour rose. 'I suppose I'm worried about Marcus.'

'Oh, is that it?' His eyes teased and her pink deepened abruptly. There was that charm in his face again and she felt herself responding to it as a flower turns to the sun, her body warming, coming alive. 'I thought something else might be on your mind,' he added, tongue in cheek, his hard mouth lifting at the corners.

'Oh, did you?' She could not hold his gaze. Her eyes flickered away and she said with a little shrug, 'I can't think what you mean.'

His soft laughter made her laugh back and their eyes met again. He put out a hand, took one of hers and lifted it to his mouth, watching her over it as his mouth slid smoothly over her wrist. 'I'll remind you at some more suitable moment,' he murmured.

When he was in this mood, she thought, he was irresistible, the strong features illumined by that smile of his, one of those secret weapons he had concealed from her for most of their early relationship.

Her heart was racing at the thought of his implied lovemaking, and he must have felt the sudden acceleration of her pulse as his lips lingered on it. He gave her a long, half-veiled look, the heavy lids hiding the expression of the grey eyes. Then the stewardess came up and he turned to speak to her, releasing Laura's hand.

They went straight from the airport to the London office, since Dan had already discovered that Marcus was there, not at his house. His mouth hardened as he turned to her after telephoning the house. 'That pigheaded old man,' he muttered. 'I told him to keep away from the office.'

'I knew he would be worried,' she said angrily, her eyes cold.

Dan surveyed her without expression. 'You don't trust me an inch, do you, Laura?'

'Not an inch,' she said in a tight voice.

'I could beat you,' he told her, turning to walk away, and she followed him with a slight frown, wondering if she had imagined the flicker of emotion in the grey eyes. Was she going mad? Or had

Dan actually looked hurt for a second before the expression faded out of his eyes?

Dan bought the evening papers at the airport and read them in the hired car, his mouth levelling in a straight line, passing them to her without a word as he finished them. She read them, paling. During the day's trading the price of their shares had shot up sharply and it was obvious that someone was buying every share that came on to the market.

'They have to be family shares,' she said bitterly. 'Most of the shares went to members of the family in the beginning and they haven't sold before.'

Dan nodded without replying.

'It isn't just Jimmy,' she said, as if excusing her father, her voice tentative. 'Aunt Dinah must have sold some. She had quite a few from my grandfather.'

'Leave it,' said Dan without looking at her.

'If Jimmy knew that the others in the family were selling ...'

He looked at her, his eyes narrowed. 'I said leave it. I realise you have a strong loyalty towards your father, but there's no need for you to make excuses for him to me. I know him.'

Yes, Laura thought, he knew Jimmy. They had worked together and Dan had made up his mind that Jimmy was a lightweight playboy, envious and spiteful, of no account. He had shouldered Jimmy out of his way without any trouble, but now Jimmy was going to upset Dan's boat and Dan would not forgive or forget it.

What could either Dan or Marcus do? she wondered. Try to outbid whoever was buying up shares? That would drain capital out of the family and put a strain upon the firm in the future.

When they walked into Dan's office Marcus was seated in his chair, bending over an open file. He looked up, starting, and gasped. 'What are you two doing back already?' He frowned at them and Laura went to his side to kiss his withered cheek, taking hold of one of the veined, gnarled hands, pressing it lovingly.

'I was worried about you.'

Marcus's eyes shot to Dan. 'What's she talking about?'

'What are you doing in the office?' Dan asked sternly. 'I thought I told you to stay at home? I left everything in Huxley's hands and the man is quite capable of managing things without supervision.'

Marcus looked guilty, like a child caught redhanded with a cookie jar. 'I couldn't stay away while all the fun was going on here,' he said sulkily. 'I wanted to be where it was all happening.'

'You could have given yourself another heart attack,' Dan scolded, but his tone had relented a little, and there was a slight smile on the cold mouth. 'Everything is going as planned. No need to rush about and flap, Marcus.'

Laura was puzzled, looking from one to the other with a frown. 'What about this take-over bid?' she demanded sharply. 'What's happening to that, Marcus?'

His eyes widened and he looked at Dan. 'She doesn't know?'

'I haven't told her yet,' he said coolly, and Laura looked at him in sudden suspicion.

'What don't I know?'

Marcus looked down at the desk, silent. Dan

studied Laura with an unreadable expression. 'I'm taking over the firm,' he said.

She was baffled. 'What's that supposed to mean? I knew that...'

'I'm buying up all the family shares,' he explained, watching her. 'I'm using my own company to do it, which is not generally known.'

Laura felt her skin grow cold. 'Your own company?'

'Dan's family firm,' said Marcus. He got up. 'I'll leave you two to talk about it. I'll be in Laura's office when you need me, Dan.' He went out slowly, then turned at the door. 'You shouldn't have interrupted your honeymoon over this, Dan. Did you have good weather?'

'Up to a point,' said Dan, still watching Laura. Marcus went out and shut the door.

Laura stood with her shoulders squared, her eyes angry. 'Well? Will you kindly tell me what this is all about? Why was I never told you had a firm of your own? What firm? What do you mean by taking over the company?'

Dan walked round and dropped into his chair, swinging idly in it. 'Sit down and listen,' he ordered as if she were some junior secretary whom he was instructing.

Her mouth shook with temper, then she sat down. 'Well?' she demanded.

'My father and his brother started a firm in the States about twenty-five years ago,' Dan began. 'They quarrelled and my father walked out. He came over here and worked in the U.K. for the rest of his life, having no contact with his brother at all. After his death my uncle got in touch with me and

I flew over and worked with him for two years, but he had a stubborn streak. He was a quarrelsome man who only saw one point of view, his own. So I walked out, just as my father had done, and for much the same reasons. Last year my uncle died and left me control of his firm. He had no children of his own. I'd just joined Belsize & Co. I could have left, but I like to finish what I've started. I didn't mean to stay more than a few months, but ...' He stopped and shrugged. 'Anyway, I stayed, but when Jimmy demanded ten per cent of the shares in return for an agreement to acquiesce in the disposal of the rest of Marcus's shares to you, I saw that at some time in the future Jimmy would upset the apple cart by selling those shares.'

Laura winced and his eyes observed her chagrin and humiliation. His mouth tightened. 'Yes, I know he's your father, but he is also a very unpredictable type. Some day I knew he would get hot under the collar over some imagined slight, then he would rush off and try to hurt me in some way by selling those shares at a difficult moment.'

Huskily, she said, 'And so you decided what?'

He shrugged. 'To precipitate things, tempt him out into the open. It seemed sensible to give myself full control, anyway, so I bought up as many shares as I could using my uncle's firm as a cloak. I deliberately chose to do this while we were out of the country. Jimmy would never suspect that I was behind it while I was on my honeymoon.'

Her eyes darkened. 'No, it sounds too coldblooded even for you,' she said coldly, and saw Dan's eyes glitter.

'Thank you,' he said curtly.

'Why did you lie to me?' she asked.

'About my uncle's firm? I suppose it was a lie by omission,' he agreed. 'But then you were so convinced that I was thirsting to get my hands on some money, weren't you? I didn't see why I should whitewash myself. You were having such fun seeing me as some sort of piranha.'

She flushed angrily. 'You let me think that there was a take-over bid, that my grandfather was under pressure ... why tell me at all?'

He smiled that blood-chilling smile of his. 'I wanted to see how you would react,' he told her.

Laura stared, dumbfounded.

'And I saw,' he said coolly. 'You at once guessed that Jimmy would sell you short. You rushed back here to protect both Marcus and your fortune.'

'What did you expect me to do? Lounge around in the sun while my grandfather fought for his company?'

Dan's eyes were inscrutable. 'Which mattered most, I wonder?'

Laura sat up straight, eyes flashing. 'The fact that you need to ask tells me exactly what you think of me!'

'That makes us even then,' he retorted. 'Because you've always made it plain what you think of me.'

She could not deny it and her teeth bit into her lower lip. 'You carefully made sure I would think the worst of you.'

'Jimmy had already laid the foundation of my black character, I imagine,' he shrugged. 'And although you seem to see his nature pretty clearly you still listen to him, don't you, Laura? I thought that night I met you in Geneva that you were very calm and unworried about his crash, but on the flight you were having a nightmare while you were asleep and I realised that under that cool little front you were a lot more concerned than you let on ... especially when I saw nailmarks in your hands ... that was a dead giveaway.'

'I don't like being spied on,' she said sharply.

'If you weren't so hung-up about being understood by those around you, it wouldn't be necessary to spy,' he said almost wearily. 'You hide too much. You're too secretive.'

She laughed sharply. 'You call me secretive!'

His mouth twitched and humour came into his eyes. 'I had to be,' he said. 'You made it clear that we were enemies from the first.'

'Weren't we?' Laura challenged him, her eyes level.

His face smoothed out, all expression gone. 'You intended that we should be, and knowing your father's view of me I wasn't sure how far I could trust you. I was getting rather sick of Jimmy's excitable animosity.' He looked at her with raised brows, his eyes cold. 'And I got very sick of yours, too.'

She clenched her hands in her lap. 'Why did you marry me?'

He was silent, watching her, then he leaned back and put his feet on the desk with a lazy stretch of the long body. 'Marcus begged me to,' he said, and watched her colour rise to a hectic scarlet.

Laura shot to her feet. 'I see.' She turned and walked to the door and he asked brusquely, 'Where are you going?'

'To my grandfather,' she said. 'Unless you have

something else to tell me.'

'For instance?' he enquired.

She gave him a bitter look. 'You aren't already married, by any chance?'

He laughed. 'Now you're being childish!'

'Sorry,' she said furiously. 'But then I'm my father's daughter.'

Dan nodded. 'I'm aware of that. I comfort myself with the thought that you're also Marcus's granddaughter and I happen to be very attached to Marcus.'

'Is that why you agreed to marry me?'

He got up slowly and sauntered over to her, standing beside her, staring at her. 'My main reason for marrying you was because I'd discovered I wanted to go to bed with you,' he drawled.

Her skin flooded with hot colour and she trembled, looking away from the too percipient eyes.

He put a hand under her hair, his fingers stroking her nape. 'At the time, I'd the idea that you led a pretty permissive existence.'

She pulled back from his caressing hand. 'You thought I was promiscuous, you mean!' Her eyes flared at him. 'I'm surprised you didn't just...' She broke off, furious with herself for what she had been about to say.

He grinned. 'Make a pass? Well, it entered my head once or twice.'

Laura remembered the way he had looked at her in the squash court, the cold exploration of her body with those hard eyes, and anger made her violent.

She raised her hand to slap him and he caught her wrist lightly, the long fingers tightening around it, biting into her. 'Temper,' he said softly. 'What did you expect? You flaunted your love life at me from the start.'

It was true, but she did not like it any the more. She wriggled her hand, trying to escape, but he held her too tightly.

'Those angry little eyes of yours made it clear that I'd get nowhere with you if I made a pass, anyway,' he drawled. 'And Marcus was so keen on the idea of a marriage between us. Why do you think he sent me to get you from Geneva?'

'You said it was your idea.'

'I lied,' he said without hesitation. 'Marcus begged me to go and even at that stage he showed pretty plainly what was in his mind. He'd been singing your praises for months, showing me photos of you, making you sound like God's gift to the male sex.'

Her eyes softened at the image of her grandfather praising her to him, blatantly selling her to Dan as a paragon.

'At first I ignored his heavy selling campaign,' Dan said drily. 'After I'd met you I found I fancied you.'

Her eyes flew to his face, her cheeks burnt. But then she had known for some time that Dan was sexually responsive to her, and it seemed to mean nothing more than a chemical reaction.

He looked down at her, releasing her hand. 'In one sense you were right about my character, Laura. I don't like being frustrated.'

She blushed. 'I remember,' she said huskily.

He grinned. 'I hope you do.' He lifted his shoulders, shrugging. 'So I married you. The night you came up to tell me you'd changed your mind and weren't going ahead with the wedding, I decided I'd take what you were so unwilling to give me, even if I had to use force.' His eyes held a little smile. 'You knocked me for six when you told me you'd never gone in for bedroom games ... that was when I saw I had to marry you, even if I had to drag you to the altar by your hair.'

Laura looked down, trembling. 'Why?' she asked him shyly.

'I've told you,' he said. 'I wanted you, and if you weren't the sort of girl I'd taken you for I couldn't take you to bed by force ... it isn't in my nature. I've never raped a girl yet.'

He had not raped her, she thought. He had seduced her with an expert comprehension of what he was doing, which indicated considerable experience.

Swallowing, she asked, 'Which leaves us where?'

He contemplated her coolly. 'Married,' he said flatly. 'And I've a strange dislike of divorce, so married we stay, Laura. It will work out. Don't pretend you found our time together disagreeable, because your response was pretty plain. Chemically, at least, we click.' He put one finger lightly on her cheek, rubbing her skin. 'It's a beginning.'

She looked up at him directly. 'I may have been inexperienced, but you weren't, were you?'

Dan's eyes narrowed, then he nodded. 'So?'

'You've made demands about my friends.'

'Demands I expect to have met,' he said. 'Laxey is out.'

'Purely as a tit-for-tat operation, so is Olivia Hamilton, then,' she said coldly.

His brows flickered. 'My secretary?'

She smiled unpleasantly at him. 'Whatever you call her.'

His lids descended, hiding his eyes. 'What do you imagine I call her?'

'It doesn't matter ... but if Joe is forbidden, so is she.'

'If you insist,' he said slowly. He gave her a wry glance. 'Want to choose my next secretary for me, by any chance?'

She grimaced at him. 'Don't be clever, Dan.' She opened the door and walked past him. Olivia Hamilton was sitting at her desk in his outer office, typing, her blonde head tilted as she read the copy on the side of the desk.

'My husband wants you,' said Laura, throwing a backward glance at Dan, her smile taunting.

His eyes were oddly amused as he met her look. Olivia got up and hurried into the office, smiling at him as she passed him. Laura went off to find her grandfather, her heart peculiarly light. Dan had not said he loved her, but he had openly admitted he found her attractive and that was something. Time might add love to his desire for her.

They had no clue as to Jimmy's whereabouts that day and Dan drove both Laura and Marcus back to Marcus's home that evening, privately telling Laura he felt they should be at hand for the next few days in case word came from Jimmy and upset Marcus. His son's strange disappearance had disturbed Marcus, although he was hiding it well. Jimmy had not sold his shares, but his absence made them all nervous.

Over breakfast next morning Marcus gave a sudden exclamation, his thin hand shaking as it held out a letter to Laura. With a quick look at his face she took it and read it hastily, making muffled sounds of amazement, irritation and amusement as she did. Dan quietly went on eating a slice of toast and marmalade, watching her.

She lowered the letter and Marcus said in exasperation, 'Isn't it typical? What can you do with him?'

'What has Jimmy been up to, then?' Dan enquired without stress, his eyes on Laura.

'He's married,' she said. 'That Sister who nursed him after the crash ... the one who came to our wedding. They were married two days after us at a register office. They're in the Bahamas on their honeymoon.'

'Jimmy isn't even aware of the take-over bid,' Marcus said with a smothered groan. 'He doesn't mention it. The letter was posted before they left the country.'

Laura held out the letter and Dan took it, throwing an eye over it rapidly. He lowered it and grimaced. 'Well, now we will have to wait and see how he does react when he gets the news. Neither you nor Laura will tell him what's going on.' He looked at Marcus. 'It would be best if Jimmy isn't aware who's buying the shares.'

Marcus nodded. 'Yes, you're right, I suppose.'

Laura bit her lip. 'You can't,' she said hurriedly. 'It's a trap ... you can't do this to him!'

Dan's face was stony. 'Marcus and I agreed that your father should have his shares now so that I could secretly buy them from him. That way he gets his money and I get the shares. What's wrong with that?'

It sounded rational, but she dimly felt that it was disloyal to her father to agree. It was a conspiracy and when Jimmy knew the truth he would feel, quite rightly, that they had all plotted against him, and he would never forgive them.

'Jimmy will be hurt,' she said, her eyes pleading with Dan.

Dan's grey eyes held hers straightly, coldly. 'Only if he deserves to be,' he said. 'If he refuses to sell we shall know we can trust him.'

'And if he sells?'

Dan's brows lifted. 'Then he's the rat I've always suspected him to be,' he said.

Marcus flinched. 'Dan!'

'My father is not a rat!' Laura snapped at the same time.

Dan glanced from one to the other with a faint, dry smile. 'You both delude yourselves. It's understandable, but shall we wait on events and see just how Jimmy does react?'

Marcus put a hand on Laura's, smiling at her wistfully. 'Dan's right, my dear ... your father is capable of it and we all know it. So we'll wait in silence, shall we?'

Laura got up from the breakfast table and walked out without a word. Dan went off to the office, surprising her, since he had said he would not spend the day there.

She went shopping in town that afternoon to buy some things for her new home and when she returned found Dan already back from the office, reading a newspaper opposite Marcus in the drawing-room. She was flushed and tired after her shopping expedition and he contemplated her without comment as she struggled into the room, her arms laden with packages.

'I got some cushion covers and that box of crystal liqueur glasses,' she told him, sinking into a chair.

He got up and removed her burden, dropping it casually on to a small table.

'Careful!' she exclaimed, sitting up straight. 'I don't want my precious crystal broken!'

Dan silently handed her a drink and she sipped it, a frown on her forehead as she looked at her grandfather who was staring at nothing. 'Something wrong?' Then her eyes flew back to Dan, who stood beside her watching her.

Her eyes widened. Huskily, she said, 'Jimmy?'

'He sold,' said Dan in cool tones.

Laura pushed the glass back into his hand and ran to Marcus, kneeling to throw her arms around him, hugging him, tears hot in her eyes. 'Oh, darling, I'm sorry!'

She could feel the hurt in the old man's body, the tension and pain. He patted her shoulder, his hands trembling. 'I knew he would, my dear,' he said threadily. 'I knew.'

She leant her head on his shoulder, holding on to him, the one sure landmark in her life until now, the only human being who had ever cared what happened to her.

'How could he?' she whispered. 'How could he do it?' Jimmy had always been unreliable, untrustworthy, but this time she felt he had stabbed her. Not knowing that Dan was behind the share-buying, he had deliberately, as he imagined, ruined the long tradition of family control. He had sold out in more ways than one, and it was herself he had betrayed, since Dan was now her husband. He had not even asked her if she would mind. He had not confided in her at all. He had just gone ahead and sold his family birthright, abandoning her.

She knew now why she had felt so disturbed at the thought that Dan was laying a trap for Jimmy. She had been afraid that Jimmy would act just as Dan had predicted. She had seen this moment of betrayal coming and had feared it.

Dan's hands took her upper arms, lifting her. Over her head he said to Marcus, 'I'll look after her.' He firmly guided her out of the room and up the stairs to their shared bedroom. She sat down on the bed, weeping bitterly, her head bent, the sleek black hair ruffled.

Dan took off her shoes, removed her dress, then held a glass of water to her lips. 'Drink this,' he said. 'And take two of these.' He shook two tablets into her palm.

Dumbly Laura obeyed him. He lifted her gently between the sheets and snapped off the light. 'Now get some sleep,' he said quietly.

She cried for a while until the drug he had given her took its effect and she slid into a deep, smothering sleep. When she woke up it was morning. She lay with half-open eyes watching the sunlight flicker along the walls like reflected water. Dust danced in a golden shower at the curtain opening.

When she went downstairs she found Marcus alone. Dan had gone to the office. 'A fine honeymoon this has turned out to be,' she said, trying to make her grandfather smile, and it did; a faint pleasure came into his red-rimmed eyes. Despite Jimmy's final betrayal, it still delighted Marcus that she had married Dan. He looked brighter as he watched her eat a slice of toast and drink some coffee.

'Why don't we drive over to the new house and look at it?' she suggested, and Marcus was eager, his eyes cheerful as he followed her to the car.

He liked the house. 'Very nice,' he agreed. 'It will suit you for a year or two. When ... well, some time you and Dan will have my place, you know. I'd like you to live there. You won't sell it, will you?' He was attached to his home. 'Your grandmother thought of it as a family home,' he said. 'She would like to know you and Dan would be living there one day with your own children.'

'Give us a chance!' she teased, laughing at him. 'We're in no hurry.'

'I am,' he said pathetically, but he smiled.

Laura felt her stomach hurting and wanted badly to bring a real light to his eyes. 'You'll be the first to know,' she promised, and he grinned.

'The second,' he suggested, and she laughed.

'The first ... after Dan.'

He laughed at that.

'Would you mind if we called him Marcus?' she asked, still wanting to please him, and he looked at her wryly.

'If it's a boy you can call it Frankenstein,' he said. 'I shan't care so long as I have a great-grandson.'

The little conversation worried and upset her. That evening she said to Dan, 'I'm concerned about Marcus. He's depressed.'

'What do you expect?' he asked her flatly. His eyes were cold. 'Are you still blaming me? I was protecting you and Marcus's firm, although I don't expect you to see it like that.'

'I wasn't getting at you,' she snapped.

'No? That makes a change.'

She retorted furiously, 'Marcus worries me. He looks as if he's letting go.'

Dan's mouth hardened. 'Do you think I hadn't noticed?'

'We can't leave him like this,' she insisted.

The grey eyes steadied on her face. 'I see. You suggest we don't move into our new home?'

She felt oddly nervous under his close stare. 'Well, we could delay it.'

'I think not,' said Dan. 'Marcus is eager for us to move in there. It may not have occurred to you, but he wants our marriage to work and he knows it's easier for a married couple to be alone in their own home.'

'In these circumstances...'

'Don't argue, Laura,' Dan said curtly. 'We move in as planned next week. I realise how desperate you are to avoid being alone with me, but you're going to have to put up with it.' Then he walked out and she stared after him, shaken because in fact he could not have been further from the truth. She wanted to be alone with him. She felt uneasy in Marcus's house, aware of his watchful eyes, but she felt it her duty to be near him.

While they were under her grandfather's roof, Dan had made no attempt to touch her, his manner when they were alone cool and polite. When they were with Marcus he seemed easier, sometimes a little teasing, his eyes smiling at her. Once or twice he had kissed her under her grandfather's approving eyes, and she had played up to him, smiling back as though she welcomed his touch.

She wondered if he was tired of playing at being a loving husband. Did he want to move into their own house so that he could drop his little advances, revert to their old guarded relationship?

They moved into the house on the day Dan had already planned. Marcus waved goodbye cheerfully, but he looked grey and old and Laura worried about him as they drove away. Left alone in the great house he would rattle around like a pea in a pod with nothing but bitter memories of Jimmy to keep him company.

Jimmy had given no indication of when he meant to return from his honeymoon, but knowing him it would no doubt be a prolonged affair.

Laura was tired the evening they moved in, so went to bed early, falling asleep quite soon. The following day Dan went off to work as usual. She had taken a further week off work to get the house in order, and stayed at home all day, working with concentration on the various little jobs which remained to be done to make the house into a habitable home.

She had expected Dan for dinner, but the hour passed and he gave no sign of returning. The food was ruined, her temper high, when at last at ten o'clock, she went up to bed. She had prepared the meal with such care, taken such care with her own appearance, that Dan's absence left her smouldering with rage.

She heard his car a quarter of an hour later and hurriedly snapped off the light. He came up the stairs and opened her door, but she lay very still, pretending to be asleep.

He did not leave, as she had expected, but came into the room and turned on the light.

'What the hell do you think you're doing?' she blazed, sitting up, glaring at him.

He came over to the bed, his hands in his pockets. 'What sort of welcome home is this?' he asked bitingly. 'You put your light off as I got back, so I knew you were awake.'

'Get out of my room!'

'The hell I will,' he retorted, his skin darkening. He sat down on the side of the bed and she caught a faint odour of whisky.

'You've been drinking!' she exclaimed, enraged further. 'Kind of you to come home at all—or had your lady-friend had enough of you?'

The heavy lids dropped. The grey eyes shone through a narrow slit, bright and cold. 'I've been dining with some American hoteliers,' he said. 'I told you that.'

'You told me nothing of the sort!'

His eyes flicked up. 'My secretary rang you!'

'Nobody rang.'

He surveyed her, brows rising. 'Nobody rang?' An odd little smile drew his mouth into a curve. 'Ah!'

'What does that mean?'

'It was Olivia's last day today,' he said softly. His eyes held amusement. 'Perhaps she forgot in the heat of the moment, but I give you my word, Laura, I asked her to ring and let you know.'

Jealousy lit inside her head like a rocket. 'Sure it was hoteliers you were dining with and not Olivia Hamilton?'

He laughed softly. 'My God, you have a nasty little mind ... no, I was not with Olivia.' He flicked her cheek with one finger. 'So get up and get me some coffee, will you?'

'I've no intention of doing any such thing,' she snapped. 'I cooked you a meal tonight. It's still in the oven if you like cold food.'

'I'm sorry, Laura,' he said, but he was still amused, she could see it in his grey eyes. 'I would much rather have come home to eat, but I couldn't get out of it.'

'I thought Dan Harland never did anything unless he wanted to!'

He stared into her eyes and his mouth toughened. 'That's right,' he said, pulling off his jacket and dropping it to the floor.

Laura's heart began to beat violently. She flew out of the bed, but Dan pulled her backwards into his arms, his mouth compelling, his hands sliding down over the silken sweep of her nightdress, and her struggle died within seconds, her arms sliding up his hard body to curl around his neck, clinging.

The light went out and she sighed deeply as she yielded. 'Is this what you want?' he whispered, pushing her back against her pillows. 'I'm sorry our first evening was ruined, Laura, but I'll make up for it now.'

She half laughed, half groaned. 'You conceited swine,' she whispered, kissing his mouth, her words breathed into it. 'I wish to heaven I could break your neck!'

He withdrew, his eyes glittering in the dark room. 'You mean you wish you could break my heart ... the way you've broken other men's, Laura.

I'm very aware of your destructive capacities, don't worry.'

She lay still, staring at his half-visible features. 'What?'

He laughed harshly. 'I've seen you at work, remember. First impressions sink deep. The night we met you had that young Swiss in tow. It was dark in your flat, but my hearing is pretty good ... it was obvious that he was crazy about you. And when he had gone it was equally obvious that you didn't give a damn. I heard you laughing.'

There was nothing she could say. It was true ... yet untrue. She was sure that Max had never been seriously in love with her. It had been as much a game to him as it had to her—but if she said so, Dan was not going to believe her.

He moved his head, his lips warmly stroking her throat. 'So I'll take whatever I can get you to give me, Laura, but don't hope to get those little claws of yours into me, because I'm tougher material than the men you've played with in the past. My heart is more durable.'

She felt a peculiar hurt, then cold anger. For a few seconds she was silent, unresponsive under his caress, then her face hardened. Dan might never love her, but she could make him want her.

She moved her head up against his cheek, her long lashes slowly tickling his skin in a butterfly kiss. 'Make love to me,' she whispered softly.

His cheek was hard against her, his body stiff, then he made a muffled sound deep in his throat and began to kiss her again, his lips searching hungrily for response.

## CHAPTER NINE

Two months later Laura was in Bond Street doing Christmas shopping, well wrapped in a fur-collared coat, her skin glowing with winter freshness. The evening was coming down, the lights of the stores gave a festive brilliance to the dark and thickening sky. A trio of music students were trailing along the gutter playing Christmas carols, the thin young violinist leading them in a Tottenham scarf, the bright flaunting colours flying over his shoulder in the wind. Laura paused to drop some coins into their outstretched tin and they all three grinned at her.

'Merry Christmas,' she said, and they shouted the words back on an impulse, including the whole street. People turned to laugh and then to fling coins to them and they looked impudently at Laura as she walked on.

The brief exchange of warmth, even between strangers, made her stupidly tearful as she pushed her way into a great department store. Her marriage was an illusion, she thought, like the image of Santa Claus up in the air above the shoppers, created from flashing lights. She and Dan behaved like husband and wife in public. Dan was clever at the mental sleight of hand which gave others the impression that he and Laura were intimately happy together. A smile, a murmured word, a glance, and she saw her friends smile at each other, totally taken in by

Dan's conjuring trick.

Marcus was the most deceived of all. Dan took extra care for him. Laura paused to frown over cufflinks, her eyes undecided. What on earth could she give Dan? It had to be something he could display to their friends, and to Marcus, yet there was so much she still did not know about the strange man who was her husband. The one thing of which she was now certain was that Dan really cared for Marcus. He took such care over her grandfather, endless trouble to see that he was happy. Every weekend they spent all their time with Marcus. Dan never seemed bored by the quiet hours he spent with the old man, and his kindness made it harder for her, showing her that beneath that cold exterior lay a heart which she might reach if she only knew the way.

Her wandering eye lit on a magnificent gold satin dressing-gown, heavily quilted and with black lapels and a tie belt.

An impish smile touched her face. Surely that would be a gift which indicated marital bliss to anyone who saw it?

She thought of Dan's surprised face and grinned to herself. He wore austere towelling wraps, not dressing-gowns, and it would undoubtedly astonish him, even if he never wore it.

Deciding to take a taxi to the station, she stood on the kerb, turning a watchful eye into the stream of homeward-bound traffic. Suddenly a prickle of instinct made her eye focus on one passing taxi, and a sick dart of anguish pierced her. Inside the cab sat Dan, an arm around Olivia Hamilton, whose blonde head lay against his shoulder.

Laura stared for a second, then turned and pushed her way among the jostling crowds, walking away with a set white face.

She had no idea where she was going. Pain made her blind to everyone she passed, everything she saw. She walked along narrow, winding streets without any sense of direction. When she emerged near the green space of Hyde Park she stood there, shivering, although her body pulsed with heat after her long walk.

The cars swept down the wide thoroughfare. Overhead the lamplight blazed orange, spilling like sunshine over the glazed shop windows and car roofs.

Sleet began to fall, cold bitter spears of it, cutting into her skin.

She went on walking, turning north, up past the great hotels with their rows of waiting taxis, passing the many foreigners who frequent that part of London, their arms full of Christmas parcels, their tongues excited, alien. In recent years the tourist season seemed to have become elastic, stretching from January to January, without a pause. London had a magnetic attraction for tourists since the shops were so full of low-priced goods of high quality.

Her body was becoming tired, but her mind was playing one scene over and over again. Dan with Olivia Hamilton sheltered protectively in his arms, his cheek against her fine golden hair.

Had he been seeing Olivia secretly throughout their marriage? Was this the tip of the iceberg?

Somehow she had come to believe that he was keeping his promise not to see Olivia. She had not seen Joe. Or anyone else, come to that. She had been idiotically, blindly faithful to Dan ever since their marriage. Although he had never so much as hinted at any sort of emotional involvement with her, he was a passionate lover. That side of their marriage worked at least. In the dark of the night they met like silent conspirators, exchanging tokens of love, if not love itself. She halted in her steps, biting her lip. All lies, she thought. What had he reduced her to, that she should be prepared to accept such a relationship?

Without realising it she seemed to have been crying. The biting whips of the sleet stung across a face wet with tears. She was very cold, very tired.

Hungry for warmth, suddenly, she hailed a passing taxi and made her way to a little Italian restaurant she knew. The owner, Luigi, came over with a broad grin. 'Long time no see ... where you been, Laura?'

'Here and there,' she said lightly. 'How are you, Luigi?'

'Busy,' he shrugged in that customary Latin fashion, graceful and wry. 'What you want to eat?'

She ordered without looking at the limited menu and he moved off. Her eyes briefly sped round the little place, not seeing the wall frescoes which she had seen so many times already, the sunlit blue seas of Italy, the cypresses and white little houses.

Warmth slowly, warily, returned to her frozen body as she drank red Chianti with her escalope. By the time she was drinking caffé espresso she was thawing out, her cheeks very flushed with the wine.

When she left the café she had made a decision. She took a taxi to Joe's flat and when he opened the door with a look of surprise she grinned at him.

'Hi, stranger!'

Joe's eyebrows drew together, but he stepped back and waved her into the flat. She took off her coat and flung it over a chair, bent to hold out her hands to the warmth of his electric log fire. 'It is freezing outside.'

'Have a drink,' said Joe, pouring her a glass of brandy.

Laura grimaced, 'Ugh!' but drank it, far too fast, while Joe watched with curious eyes.

'What's wrong?' he asked her quietly.

She turned and came to sit beside him on the long orange sofa which took up most of the room. Leaning back, she closed her eyes with a sigh, 'Everything,' she said flatly.

He picked up one of her hands and rubbed it gently between both his, asking, 'Come on, Laura. You can tell me.'

'Don't ask, Joe. Let me just sit here for a while. It's so cold outside.'

'And inside, judging by your eyes,' he said in anxious tones.

Yes, she thought. Icy, freezing cold which invaded every nerve of her body. She had felt, as she walked, that she was totally alone in a hostile, empty world, and this was the only place she could think of where she might be safe for a while.

'I might be able to help,' Joe said.

'Nobody can,' she muttered, opening her eyes and giving him a faint smile almost of apology. 'I had no business coming here, inflicting this on you.'

'We're friends,' Joe said. His eyes were firm and unwavering. 'Aren't we, Laura? Obviously it's something to do with Harland. That husband of yours is a pretty icy chap. What's he done to you?'

Before she could reply, the telephone rang and Joe grimaced and got up to answer it. His face altered as he listened to whoever was on the other end of the line. He glanced quickly at Laura and she sat up, sensing that it was Dan. Joe held the phone out to her, saying nothing, and she slowly took it, her skin deathly white.

'Yes?' she asked drily.

There was a silence, then Dan said curtly, 'Marcus has had another attack ... can you get down here right away?' Before she could reply he had replaced his own receiver with a crash which hurt her eardrums. She spoke hoarsely, as if he could still hear her, a bitter question in her voice, 'Marcus?' Then, realising her own stupidity, she put down the phone and turned to Joe, shivering. 'It's Marcus.'

'I know,' he said quietly. 'Harland said as much.'

'It's my fault,' she said in a half frantic way. 'My fault.' She felt guilty, as though by wishing her marriage ended she had somehow brought on Marcus's attack. Marcus had wished for the marriage and her conscience began to reproach her, plucking at her nerves. Tears sprang into her eyes and Joe saw them with a click of the tongue, patting her trembling shoulder.

'Now then, don't give up heart ... he's come through these attacks before. I'll drive you down, Laura.' He got his coat and buttoned her into her own, pushing aside her trembling fingers as if she were a child.

They drove in a heavy silence through the sleet, the windscreen wipers flashing to and fro across her angle of vision, giving her a peculiar aching behind her eyes, as though she were about to have a migraine.

'Shall I come in with you?' Joe asked as they reached the house.

Laura shook her head. 'Better not.'

He looked distinctly relieved and, despite her misery, she felt a brief wry amusement and smiled at him. 'Poor Joe, I'm sorry to have dragged you into this ... especially on such a night.'

'What are friends for?' he asked. She bent over and kissed him lightly on the cheek.

'Thanks, Joe.'

The front door opened and light spilled out over the dark pathway, shining through the slashing spears of sleet. Laura got out of the car and Joe drove away. Turning, she found herself facing Dan, his face a cold mask.

'How is he?' she asked, walking towards him anxiously.

'In hospital,' Dan said with a curious, clipped ring.

She halted. 'Why aren't you there? We must go at once!'

'There's nothing we can do,' he said in a tone so final that she felt her body wince with horror.

'He ... are you saying ...' She could not voice the unacceptable possibility his words had conjured up in her mind. She glared at him angrily, bitterness invading her.

'The doctors have got him in an intensive care unit, but all we could do is sit and wait, which we might as well do here.'

Her breath came out in a thick, relieved sigh. 'He's alive, then.'

'It's touch and go this time,' said Dan. He glanced up at the dark sky. 'Come inside, for God's sake. You're getting soaked.'

Laura walked into the dark hall as he switched off the porch light. He took off her coat as she finished unbuttoning it and she walked into the lit sitting-room.

Turning, she asked, 'What happened?'

Dan lifted his wide shoulders. 'Apparently he got a phone call from Jimmy.'

'Jimmy!' Her voice shot out angrily. 'He's back?'

Dan shook his head. 'He isn't coming back. I knew that. He's bought a house over in the Bahamas and is planning to stay there for good. I hadn't told Marcus because I thought it was safer to keep him in the dark for a while. Marcus was still hoping Jimmy would come back.' He gave her an unreadable look. 'Your grandfather is an optimist where his black sheep of a son is concerned.'

Laura felt bitter rage against her father. 'But Jimmy rang. What did he say?'

Dan shrugged. 'God knows. Mrs Jacques took the call at first, then Jimmy spoke to Marcus. Mrs Jacques heard Marcus cry out and when she ran in he was collapsed on the floor. She's a quick-thinking woman, she rang for an ambulance at once and got him to hospital, then she rang me.'

She walked to and fro in front of the great roaring fire, wringing her hands in a distracted, angry fashion. 'How could Jimmy do it? How can anyone be so selfish? He's never been an admirable character, but he seems to get worse as he gets older!'

Dan moved to the decanter on a tray behind the brocade sofa and she heard the swish of whisky.

'Drink it,' he said, putting it into her cold hands.

She pushed it away, shaking her head. 'I hate the stuff.'

'Drink it,' he ordered, lips compressed, giving her a long stare from the icy grey eyes.

'Why don't you leave me alone?' she burst out furiously, her colour mounting suddenly, her blue eyes dark with temper.

'You're my wife,' he said, his tone oddly deliberate, and her cheeks burnt a bitter scarlet.

'Only while Marcus is alive,' she flung at him, and hearing the words knew that that had been in her mind all day. It was why she had been so self-reproachful when she heard of his attack. She had felt at once that she had almost wished it, although her conscious brain told her firmly that nothing could have hurt her more.

Dan's face tightened, a muscle jerking in his flat cheek. 'Ah,' he said through those hard lips, 'I wondered when we would come to that.'

Laura bit her lower lip, nerving herself for a reply, and his eyes watched her narrowly. She saw that he knew exactly what was in her mind.

'This is no time to talk about it,' she said huskily. 'Later.' She drew a shaky breath. 'No, it must wait.' She could not bear to take part in any such discussion at this moment, while Marcus lay fighting for life in a hospital ward.

Dan poured himself a drink and swallowed half of it rapidly, his eyes fixed on the orange flames leaping up the chimney. The wind howled against the windows, making them rattle. Sleet suddenly blew down the chimney and hissed into the fire.

He put down his glass with a thud which made

Laura jump. She looked at him warily. He was staring at her now with angry little flames leaping in the grey eyes, their ice dissolving in a conflagration of sheer rage. 'We'll talk about it now,' he said sharply.

'No,' she denied, turning towards the door.

He took three quick strides, barring her way, his back against the door. 'Let's have it,' he said curtly.

'We both know that this is not the time to talk about it,' she said bitterly. 'But if you insist.' She moved backwards, finding his nearness intolerable. 'Ours was a marriage of convenience, and of Marcus dies the reason for it will no longer exist.'

Although his face was rigid, a fierce cold mask, she felt an indefinable menace emanating from him as he stared at her, his eyes narrowed.

There was a silence for a moment, then he said icily, 'How often have you seen Laxey since our marriage?'

She flushed more deeply, but met his stare without wavering. 'Only today,' she said in flat tones.

His brows lifted, cold mockery in the look he gave her. 'You expect me to believe that?'

'It's the truth. Believe it or not as you like.'

'I trusted you,' he said contemptuously. 'I believed you were no longer seeing him.'

'We made a bargain,' she reminded him bitterly. 'I wouldn't see Joe if you didn't see Olivia ... you broke it first.'

For a moment his face was quite still, his eyes slits of grey ice. Then he asked slowly, 'What do you mean?'

She laughed angrily. 'That surprised you, didn't it? Yes, I know you've seen her ... you saw her today, didn't you?' Her eyes held stinging scorn. 'Yet you stand there accusing me as if you were entitled to point a finger!'

He pushed his hands into his pockets, rocking back on his heels. 'I had lunch with Olivia today,' he agreed. He watched her. 'And her fiancé.'

Laura felt a shock run through her. She stared, colour fading. 'Her fiancé?'

'You hadn't heard?' He was filled with a cold mockery now, his mouth sharp with distaste. 'Yes, Olivia is getting married after Christmas to an Australian she met a couple of months ago—a whirlwind romance. Our lunch was pretty hectic ... I'm afraid Olivia indulged in too much champagne and afterwards her fiancé had a business appointment, so I agreed to take her back to her flat. She was in no condition to see herself home. Her mother was staying with her, though, so I dropped her into Mama's cross arms and shot off home.' His eyes flashed to her face and there was open rage in them. 'To my loving, faithful wife!'

Laura backed, suddenly aware of real menace in that cold face. Under Dan's controlled exterior she could now feel a smouldering temper which alarmed her.

'Don't run away,' he said silkily. 'What were you doing at Laxey's flat?'

She ran a quivering tongue tip over her dry mouth. 'Talking,' she said huskily.

'Tit for tat, you little bitch?' he asked, moving towards her. 'And how far did your ideas of revenge on me go, Laura?'

Answering the look in his eyes rather than his words, she muttered, 'No, I didn't.'

Dan loomed over her, his black head bent. 'You are never going to Laxey,' he said through his teeth. 'Never, do you hear?' His eyes flamed between their heavy lids. 'I told you I would break him if you tried and I meant it. I've already smashed his plates.'

Her eyes opened wide, horror and incredulity in them. 'You've done what?'

'After I'd spoken to you at his flat I threw them out,' he said coolly. 'You'll find the pieces in the dustbin.'

'Why?' she gasped. 'Those beautiful things ... how could you?'

His hand snaked out and caught her upper arm, jerking her towards him. 'I couldn't get my hands on Laxey at the time, so I took the next best step.'

Her heart began to beat heavily against her breastbone. She could not hold his stare. 'They were priceless,' she whispered.

'Go to Laxey and I'll ruin him if it takes every penny I've got in the world,' he said in a taut, stiff voice.

Laura turned her head away, trembling. She felt confused, incredulous, as though the scene were something in a dream.

'Aren't you curious to know why?' Dan asked in that harsh voice. 'Look at me, Laura!'

Her lashes flickered against her hot cheeks, but she could not voice a word, or move, staring at the floor.

'Tell me the truth,' he said. 'Are you in love with Laxey?'

Silently she shook her head, her mouth dry.

His hand moved over her shoulder, his thumb

almost absently stroking her collarbone in a slow caress.

'Laugh, Laura,' he said thickly. 'I can't hide it any longer. For the first time in my life I'm at the mercy of another human being and I don't find the experience very enjoyable.' He shook her, both hands locking on her shoulders. 'Well, laugh, damn you!'

She hung in his hands like a doll, her eyes lifting to his face, a passionate question in them. 'What are you saying?'

She was looking at the darkly passionate face of a lover, his eyes tormented, his mouth wry with compressed intensity.

'You know damned well what I'm saying,' he muttered through his teeth.

'Just tell me,' she whispered, suddenly lightheaded, provocatively teasing, her smile coming like the rainbow after storm, the blue eyes wide and inviting.

One hand came up to close around her nape, sliding into the silky black strands of her hair, caressing her skin. 'I'm not exposing myself any more than I have already,' he said in a savage voice.

She felt the blood racing around her body as though some long ice age were coming to an end, a thaw setting in, the onset of it giving her an unexpected, unlooked-for hope. Dan's reluctance to put his feelings into words was convincing. Even more convincing was the thickness of his breathing as he bent towards her, his mouth beginning to caress her ears, her chin, her cheeks.

Her hands slid up his chest and he drew back to look at her, his eyes on her parted lips.

'I love you,' she whispered.

She heard the hard intake of his breath, then he crushed her against him, finding her mouth savagely, the violence and need of long-denied love like flame between them. She clung to him, winding her arms around his neck, sensual hunger in the eager response of her mouth under his, her fingers clenching in the thick black hair, pulling his head down.

After a while he held her away, staring down into her face with eyes which ate her. 'Say it again,' he said huskily. 'I can't believe it.'

Her eyes were dark with passion, her hands still weaving through his hair. 'I love you,' she said with a sigh.

'Then why did you threaten to leave me?'

'I thought you loved Olivia,' she admitted. 'I couldn't bear to stay imagining that you were her lover.'

'Olivia!' His snort of irritation was convincing. 'My God, girl, I could have married her years ago if I'd ever been in love with her, but we've never been anything but good friends. She's a first-class secretary.

'I hate her,' said Laura, openly childish, her eyes smouldering.

Dan laughed then, the taut lines of his face relaxing. 'Jealous, my darling? I can't pretend to be sorry. I was so jealous of Laxey I could have killed him at one stage ... before I discovered that he'd never been your lover, I really detested him.'

She leaned her body against him, sighing. 'Dan, darling...'

He buried his face against her throat, kissing it hotly. 'I love you,' he murmured into her skin, and she sensed that even now he was reluctant to speak the words openly. 'I love you, Laura.'

'Why have you always been so cold to me?' she whispered.

'It was my own form of self-defence,' he grimaced. 'You had me in a tizzy from the day we met—but remember I thought you were a promiscuous little siren. The last thing I wanted was for you to know you'd knocked me for six.'

'Why did you deliberately let me think the worst of you?' she asked curiously.

He gave her a look which held taunting amusement. 'It seemed to be what you preferred to believe,' he shrugged. 'You saw me as some sort of financial pirate from the start.'

'Not exactly,' she challenged, her eyes glinting. 'I saw you as a frozen statue of a man. Poor Renata ... she really found you alarming that evening!'

'I was tired after the plane journey,' he admitted. 'And worried about Marcus.'

'Not to mention irritated at his blatant plans to marry you off to his unknown granddaughter,' she guessed impudently, teasing him.

He grinned down at her. 'At first, yes, I was furious. It wasn't long, though, before I was obsessed with the idea and then I came up against your obvious dislike of me. If I'd known your affairs were all so singularly platonic I would have turned on the heat much earlier. But I've never fancied the idea of queueing up for any woman. While you were apparently giving your favours to Laxey and that puppy Rees, I had no wish to stake any claim. I had to get desperate before I was ready to admit to myself that I had to have you, other men or not.'

Laura laughed, her blue eyes adoring. 'There

was never anyone before, Dan. I've never been in love with anyone.' Her face sobered. 'In fact, the idea of it scared me rigid! I hated the idea of falling in love because it seemed to me that it just left you open to pain and humiliation. Even when I had to admit I was falling in love with you, I resented it.'

'Do you still resent it?' he asked, a slight frown on his face, watching her closely.

She took a deep breath. 'If you love me, no,' she murmured, her voice shaking.

'If!' His eyes flared, a darkly passionate expression in them. 'My God, woman, what do you want me to do to prove it?' He brought his mouth down, hard, bruising her lips apart, a hungry need in his own, and she felt urgency burning deep in her body. They pressed closer, his strong thighs hard against her own. She abandoned the last shreds of her self-defence, giving herself without reserve to his demanding caresses. She heard him groaning, his hands moving faster down her curved body.

The telephone broke them apart. For a few seconds Dan looked almost bewildered, the taut mask of his face dazed. Then he moved away and she heard him ask curtly, 'Yes?'

She smoothed down the tangle into which his wandering hands had flung her hair. Dan's face changed. His voice was warmer, softer. She turned to listen, alert.

He put down the phone and gave her a triumphant grin. 'Marcus has begun to pick up ... he's responding to a new drug they're giving him, and they say his heartbeat is stronger.'

She sighed deeply. 'Thank God!'

'That grandfather of yours is stronger than he

looks,' Dan said, but his own relief and pleasure was apparent in his grey eyes. 'It will take something bigger than Jimmy to stop Marcus!'

'All the same, these attacks can't continue,' Laura said wearily. 'How much of this can he take?'

Dan came over and slid his hands around her waist, holding her gently against him. 'We could always give him something to take his mind off Jimmy,' he murmured, watching her wickedly.

She raised her eyes to his face. 'What?' she asked unwarily.

'A great grandson,' Dan said very mockingly, and saw the colour run into her cheeks.

She laughed. 'Why, you ...'

His mouth cut off the words and, gasping under the possessive fire of his lips, she realised that the way Dan could make her feel was worth all the pain he had caused her in the past. Love was a circle— her love and need went to Dan and his to her, completing the electrical circuit linking them, flowing round and round between them.

He lifted her into his arms. 'Let's hope Mrs Jacques is still resting in her room,' he whispered into her ear. 'She went off there just before you arrived. She'd had a bad shock, so we must hope it will keep her out of the way for a few hours.'

Laura laughed and struggled faintly. 'Dan, we can't ...'

'Who can't?' he asked, carrying her up the stairs.

In the dark warm bedroom they lay in each other's arms, kissing with the deep urgency of a passion at last admitted. Dan held her, looking down into her eyes, a smile on his hard mouth which took her breath away. Gone was the coldness which she had thought he would always wear towards her. In his eyes burnt a love and passion which was deeper than anything she had ever dreamt of.

'I wish this was the first day of our marriage,' she murmured, and he smiled at her.

'It is,' he said deeply. 'The first time I've ever held you in my arms and known for certain that it was where you wanted to be.'

'I think I've wanted to be in your arms since the first night we met,' she said in self-mockery. 'I fought it, but I was a push-over for you, Dan, from the moment I saw you.'

It had been a long battle and she had lost most of their encounters. She thought of the brilliant blue light on the road to Epidaurus where Dan had first kissed her, remembering the impact on herself of the cold touch of his hard mouth. It had been at that moment that she had admitted to herself just how much she wanted him, but even then she had never realised that the love she was so reluctant to believe in might one day come to dominate her whole world.

'When you said my name in the theatre at Epidaurus I was terrified,' she laughed. 'You made it sound like a blood-curdling threat!'

His eyes mocked her. 'It was, my darling. I was right behind you and you knew it. I meant you to know I wanted you.'

Laura had always seen love as a black void, but in his arms she saw that the smothering darkness she had always dreaded was only the gateway. Dan was huskily muttering words of love into her ear, kissing her neck, his breathing thick with passion.

'I love you,' she cried, hoarse submission in her voice, and plunged at last into the final freedom which love's possession held out if one first submitted to the little death which went before.

# Titles available this month in the Mills & Boon ROMANCE Series

**SENTIMENTAL JOURNEY** by *Janet Dailey*
Jessica found no difficulty at all in responding to Brodie Hayes's devastating attraction — but could she ever be anything but a substitute for her beautiful sister Jordanna?

**TEMPTED BY DESIRE** by *Carole Mortimer*
Vidal Martino was the man of Suzanne's dreams — so why couldn't her bitchy stepmother transfer her attention away from Vidal to his even richer brother Cesare?

**CLOSE TO THE HEART** by *Rebecca Stratton*
Lisa had crossed swords with the formidable Yusuf ben Dacra — but he had turned the tables on her and now she was completely in his power.

**CASTLE OF THE FOUNTAINS** by *Margaret Rome*
Visiting Sicily, Rosalba discovered that the old custom of vendetta was by no means dead — not as long as Salvatore Diavolo had anything to do with it!

**THE SHEIK'S CAPTIVE** by *Violet Winspear*
'If you save a life, you own it,' the Sheik Khasim ben Haran had told Diane — and he had saved her from the heat of the desert...

**THE VITAL SPARK** by *Angela Carson*
It was obvious to Lee that Haydn Scott intended to take over her family business — was he going to take her over as well?

**MOONLIGHT ON THE NILE** by *Elizabeth Ashton*
Working in Egypt, Lorna had fallen in love with the mysterious Miles Faversham. But was she right to trust her heart and her whole future to him?

**POSSESSION** by *Charlotte Lamb*
Laura was horribly afraid that Dan Harland didn't just want possession of the family firm; he wanted her too...

**PACT WITHOUT DESIRE** by *Jane Arbor*
Sara had rashly accepted Rede Forrest's proposal of marriage, and she hadn't anticipated all the emotional problems what would arise...

**THE JADE GIRL** by *Daphne Clair*
What was it about Alex Lines that made Stacy so resentful when he came to live in her home for a few weeks?

## Mills & Boon Romances
*— all that's pleasurable in Romantic Reading!*

Available August 1979

## Also available this month
## Four Titles in our Mills & Boon
## Classics Series

*Specially chosen reissues of the best in Romantic Fiction*

August's Titles are:

### HUNTER OF THE EAST
*by Anne Hampson*

Kim's flighty young foster-sister was about to ruin her life by running off with a married man, and Kim had to do something drastic to stop her. She declared that the only thing to do was to kidnap the man in question. Unfortunately, Kim kidnapped the wrong man...

### TIME OF CURTAINFALL
### (Darling Rhadamanthus!)
*by Margery Hilton*

After her father died, Judy was somewhat daunted to find that he had consigned her to the guardianship of his old friend the forbidding Quentin Frayle. Then she found that there was a far more attractive side to him — and alas! it was all being turned on his glamorous cousin Crystal.

### BAUHINIA JUNCTION
*by Margaret Way*

"You know, Gena," the cattle baron Cy Brandt told her, "there's the same easy magic in handling women as horses. Just show 'em who's master!" There was no doubt that Cy was good at handling horses, considered Gena, but as far as women were concerned, he had only just made her own acquaintance — and he would be in for a surprise.

### DESERT DOCTOR
*by Violet Winspear*

It seemed as if the Lawrence-like Doctor Victor Tourelle must be a hundred per cent proof against young secretaries like Madeline. And yet he seemed interested in Donette, who was only one year older. But even if the Frenchman was out of her reach, Madeline could not stop herself hoping.

**BUY THEM TODAY**

# Forthcoming Mills & Boon Romances

**RETURN TO DEVIL'S VIEW** by *Rosemary Carter*
Jana could only succeed in her search for some vital information by working as secretary to the enigmatic Clint Dubois — and it was clear that Clint suspected her motives...

**THE MAN ON THE PEAK** by *Katrina Britt*
The last thing Suzanne had wanted or expected when she went to Hong Kong for a holiday was to run into her ex-husband Raoul...

**TOGETHER AGAIN** by *Flora Kidd*
Ellen and Dermid Craig had separated, but now circumstances had brought Ellen back to confront Dermid again. Was this her chance to rebuild her marriage, or was it too late?

**A ROSE FROM LUCIFER** by *Anne Hampson*
Colette had always loved the imposing Greek Luke Marlis, but only now was he showing that he was interested in her. Interested — but not, it seemed, enough to want to marry her...

**THE JUDAS TRAP** by *Anne Mather*
When Sara Fortune fell in love with Michael Tregower, and he with her, all could have ended happily. Had it not been for the secret that Sara dared not tell him...

**THE TEMPESTUOUS FLAME** by *Carole Mortimer*
Caroline had no intention of marrying Greg Fortnum, whom she didn't even know apart from his dubious reputation — so she escaped to Cumbria where she met the mysterious André...

**WITH THIS RING** by *Mary Wibberley*
Siana had no memory of who she really was. But what were Matthew Craven's motives when he appeared and announced that he was going to help her find herself again?

**SOLITAIRE** by *Sara Craven*
The sooner Marty got away from Luc Dumarais the better, for Luc was right out of her league, and to let him become important to her would mean nothing but disaster...

**SWEET COMPULSION** by *Victoria Woolf*
Marcy Campion was convinced that she was right not to let Randal Saxton develop her plot of land — if only she could be equally convinced about her true feelings for Randal!

**SHADOW OF THE PAST** by *Robyn Donald*
Morag would have enjoyed going back to Wharuaroa, where she had been happy as a teenager, if it hadn't meant coming into constant contact with Thorpe Cunningham.

Available September 1979

# Forthcoming Classic Romances

### DARK ENEMY
*by Anne Mather*

Determined to revenge herself on Jason Wilde because of the way he had treated her sister, Nicola took a job with the oil company Jason worked for. To achieve her purpose, she determined to make him attracted to her. But things did not quite work out in the manner she expected.

### MY HEART'S A DANCER
*by Roberta Leigh*

Melanie's marriage had ended before it had begun — but happily it was not long before she found herself in love once again. Yet even now happiness looked like eluding her, when her career as a ballet dancer began to come between her and the man she loved.

### SECRET HEIRESS
*by Eleanor Farnes*

Young love is a pretty sight; but is it always strong and durable? Fiona's father had his doubts, and that was why he arranged for her to see a little of life outside her own small circle before becoming engaged to Guy. Would the experiment be successful, or might it lead her into real unhappiness?

### THE PAGAN ISLAND
*by Violet Winspear*

In an effort to forget her grief over her beloved Dion's death, Hebe had gone to the lovely Greek island of Petra. There she met Nikos Stephanos, a man as different from Dion as he could possibly be. But a dark tragedy lay over Nikos's life. Would he bring tragedy to Hebe as well?

## Mills & Boon Classic Romances

*— all that's best in Romantic Reading*

Available September 1979

**CUT OUT AND POST THIS PAGE TO RECEIVE**

# FREE FULL COLOUR Mills & Boon CATALOGUE

and – if you wish – why not also ORDER NOW any (or all) of the favourite titles offered overleaf?

Because you've enjoyed *this* Mills & Boon romance so very much, you'll really *love* choosing more of your favourite romantic reading from the fascinating, sparkling full-colour pages of "Happy Reading" – the *complete* Mills & Boon catalogue. It not only lists ALL our current top-selling love stories, but it also brings you *advance news* of all our exciting NEW TITLES *plus* lots of super SPECIAL OFFERS! And it comes to you complete with a convenient, easy-to-use DIRECT DELIVERY Order Form.

Imagine! No more *waiting*! No more "sorry – sold out" disappointments! HURRY! Send for *your* FREE Catalogue NOW ... and ensure a REGULAR supply of all your best-loved Mills & Boon romances this happy, carefree, DIRECT DELIVERY way! But why wait?

Why not – *at the same time* – ORDER NOW a few of the highly recommended titles listed, for your convenience, *overleaf?* It's so simple! Just tick *your* selection(s) on the back and complete the coupon below. Then post *this whole page* – with your remittance (including correct postage and packing) for speedy *by-return* despatch.

✱**POST TO: MILLS & BOON READER SERVICE, P.O. Box 236, Thornton Road, Croydon, Surrey CR9 3RU, England.**

*Please tick ✓ (as applicable) below:–*

☐ Please send me the FREE Mills & Boon Catalogue

☐ As well as my FREE Catalogue please send me the title(s) I have ticked ✓ overleaf

I enclose £............... (No C.O.D.) Please ADD 18p if only ONE book is ordered. If TWO (or more) are ordered please ADD just 10p per book. MAXIMUM CHARGE 60p if SIX (or more) books are ordered.

*Please write in BLOCK LETTERS below*

NAME (Mrs./Miss)..................................................

ADDRESS ..............................................................

CITY/TOWN............................................................

COUNTY/COUNTRY........................... POSTAL/ZIP CODE...........

✱ *S.African and Rhodesian readers please write to:* P.O. Box 11190, Johannesburg, 2000, S.Africa.

**ORDER NOW FOR DIRECT DELIVERY**

*Choose from this selection of*

## Mills & Boon FAVOURITES
*—ALL HIGHLY RECOMMENDED*

- ☐ 1501 **THE SILKEN TRAP** *Charlotte Lamb*
- ☐ 1502 **THE MIDNIGHT SUN** *Katrina Britt*
- ☐ 1503 **A VERY SPECIAL MAN** *Marjorie Lewty*
- ☐ 1504 **WIFE IN EXCHANGE** *Robyn Donald*
- ☐ 1505 **BEHIND A CLOSED DOOR** *Jane Donnelly*
- ☐ 1506 **BRIDE FOR A NIGHT** *Anne Hampson*
- ☐ 1507 **THE AWAKENING** *Rosemary Carter*
- ☐ 1508 **STRANGER ON THE BEACH** *Lilian Peake*
- ☐ 1509 **SUN AND CANDLELIGHT** *Betty Neels*
- ☐ 1510 **SUMMER RAINFALL** *Kerry Allyne*
- ☐ 1511 **THE PLAINS OF PROMISE** *Kerry Allyne*
- ☐ 1512 **MY LADY OF THE FUCHSIAS** *Essie Summers*
- ☐ 1513 **ONLY YOU** *Margaret Pargeter*
- ☐ 1514 **KOWHAI COUNTRY** *Gloria Bevan*
- ☐ 1515 **THE DARK WARRIOR** *Mary Wibberley*
- ☐ 1516 **CANADIAN AFFAIR** (Holiday Affair) *Flora Kidd*
- ☐ 1517 **LOW COUNTRY LIAR** *Janet Dailey*
- ☐ 1518 **SHATTERED DREAMS** *Sally Wentworth*
- ☐ 1519 **DARK MASTER** *Charlotte Lamb*
- ☐ 1520 **FORESTS OF THE DRAGON** *Rosemary Carter*

**ONLY 55p EACH**

SIMPLY TICK ☑ YOUR SELECTION(S) ABOVE, THEN JUST COMPLETE AND POST THE ORDER FORM OVERLEAF ▶